More Than Possess You

Also From Shayla Black

CONTEMPORARY ROMANCE

WICKED & DEVOTED
Wicked as Sin (Brea & One-Mile, part 1)
Wicked Ever After (Brea & One-Mile, part 2)
Wicked as Lies (Zyron & Tessa, part 1)
Wicked and True (Zyron & Tessa, part 2)
Coming Soon:
Wicked as Seduction (Trees & Laila, part 1) (March 15, 2022)

REED FAMILY RECKONING

SIBLINGS
More Than Want You (Maxon & Keeley)
More Than Need You (Griff & Britta)
More Than Love You (Harlow & Noah)

BASTARDS
More Than Crave You (Evan & Nia)
More Than Tempt You (Bethany & Clint)

FRIENDS
More Than Pleasure You (Stephen & Skye)
More Than Dare You (Trace & Masey)
More Than Protect You (Amanda & Tanner)
More Than Possess You (A Hope Series crossover) (Echo & Hayes)
Coming Soon:
More Than Hate You (October 12, 2021) (Sebastian & Sloan)

FORBIDDEN CONFESSIONS (Sexy Bedtime Stories)

FIRST TIME (Complete Series)
Seducing the Innocent
Seducing the Bride
Seducing the Stranger
Seducing the Enemy

PROTECTORS (Complete Series)
Seduced by the Bodyguard
Seduced by the Spy
Seduced by the Assassin
Seduced by the Mafia Boss

FILTHY RICH BOSSES
Tempted by the Billionaire

THE WICKED LOVERS (Complete Series)
Wicked Ties
Decadent
Delicious
Surrender To Me
Belong To Me
Wicked to Love
Mine To Hold
Wicked All The Way
Ours To Love
Wicked All Night
Forever Wicked
Theirs To Cherish
His to Take
Pure Wicked
Wicked for You
Falling in Deeper
Dirty Wicked
A Very Wicked Christmas
Holding on Tighter

THE DEVOTED LOVERS (Complete Series)
Devoted to Pleasure
Devoted to Wicked
Devoted to Love

THE UNBROKEN SERIES (by Shayla Black and Jenna Jacob)

RAINE FALLING
The Broken

The Betrayal
The Break
The Brink
The Bond

HEAVENLY RISING
The Choice
The Chase
The Commitment

THE PERFECT GENTLEMEN (by Shayla Black and Lexi Blake) (Complete Series)
Scandal Never Sleeps
Seduction in Session
Big Easy Temptation
Smoke and Sin
At the Pleasure of the President

MASTERS OF Ménage (by Shayla Black and Lexi Blake)
Their Virgin Captive
Their Virgin's Secret
Their Virgin Concubine
Their Virgin Princess
Their Virgin Hostage
Their Virgin Secretary
Their Virgin Mistress

SEXY STANDALONES
Naughty Little Secret
Watch Me
Dirty and Dangerous
Her Fantasy Men – Four Play Anthology
A Perfect Match

THE HOPE SISTERS
Misadventures of a Backup Bride
Misadventures with My Ex
More Than Possess You (A Reed Family Reckoning crossover)

More Than Possess You

A More Than Words Novella

By Shayla Black

1001 DARK NIGHTS

PRESS

More Than Possess You: A More Than Words Novella
Copyright 2021 Shelley Bradley LLC
ISBN: 978-1-951812-51-5

Foreword: Copyright 2014 M. J. Rose

Published by 1001 Dark Nights Press, an imprint of Evil Eye Concepts, Incorporated

Sign up for the 1001 Dark Nights Newsletter
and be entered to win a Tiffany Key necklace.

There's a contest every month!

Go to www.1001DarkNights.com to subscribe.

**As a bonus, all subscribers can download
FIVE FREE exclusive books!**

One Thousand and One Dark Nights

Once upon a time, in the future...

*I was a student fascinated with stories and learning.
I studied philosophy, poetry, history, the occult, and
the art and science of love and magic. I had a vast
library at my father's home and collected thousands
of volumes of fantastic tales.*

*I learned all about ancient races and bygone
times. About myths and legends and dreams of all
people through the millennium. And the more I read
the stronger my imagination grew until I discovered
that I was able to travel into the stories... to actually
become part of them.*

*I wish I could say that I listened to my teacher
and respected my gift, as I ought to have. If I had, I
would not be telling you this tale now.
But I was foolhardy and confused, showing off
with bravery.*

*One afternoon, curious about the myth of the
Arabian Nights, I traveled back to ancient Persia to
see for myself if it was true that every day Shahryar
(Persian: شهريار, "king") married a new virgin, and then
sent yesterday's wife to be beheaded. It was written
and I had read that by the time he met Scheherazade,
the vizier's daughter, he'd killed one thousand
women.*

*Something went wrong with my efforts. I arrived
in the midst of the story and somehow exchanged
places with Scheherazade — a phenomena that had
never occurred before and that still to this day, I
cannot explain.*

*Now I am trapped in that ancient past. I have
taken on Scheherazade's life and the only way I can
protect myself and stay alive is to do what she did to
protect herself and stay alive.*

*Every night the King calls for me and listens as I spin tales.
And when the evening ends and dawn breaks, I stop at a
point that leaves him breathless and yearning for more.
And so the King spares my life for one more day, so that
he might hear the rest of my dark tale.*

*As soon as I finish a story... I begin a new
one... like the one that you, dear reader, have before
you now.*

Playlist

There are infinite ways to tell someone you love them. Some of the most powerful don't require words at all. This was the truth rolling through my head when I first conceived of this series, writing about a love so complete that mere letters strung together to make sentences weren't an adequate communicator of those feelings. Instead, for this series, music was my go-to choice.

I *love* music. I'm always immersed in it and spend hours a day with my ear buds plugged in. I write to music. I think to music. I even sleep to music. I was thrilled to incorporate songs into the story I felt were meaningful to the journey. I think of it this way: a movie has a soundtrack. Why shouldn't a book?

So I created one.

Some of the songs I've selected will be familiar. Some are old. Some are newer. Some popular. Some obscure. They all just fit (in my opinion) and came straight from the heart. I listened to many of these songs as I wrote the book.

For maximum understanding (and feels), I seriously recommend becoming familiar with these songs and either playing them or rolling them around in your head as you read. I've also made it simple for you to give these songs a listen by creating a Spotify playlist.

Hugs and happy reading!

1000 Times - Sara Bareilles
I Like It - Cardi B and J Balvin
Hot In Here - Nelly
Walking on Sunshine - Katrina & the Waves
Watermelon Sugar - Harry Styles

Chapter One

Hayes

"Hey, shortcake." I wink at my best friend as she opens the door to her stamp-size studio apartment, wearing a white, gauzy, hippy-dippy-trippy halter top and matching shorts with hanging tassels and crocheted lace. Whoa. I've never seen her bare that much skin—shoulders, midriff, and thighs—but the style is definitely her vibe. The outfit, like the light brown waves she's swept from her face in a casual tangle of braids, must be how she's coping with the strong, hot spring suddenly gripping LA.

But I shouldn't be surprised by anything Echo Hope says or does. I learned long ago to expect the unexpected from my bestie.

"Hey, string bean." She steps back to let me in, the strains of some chick ballad playing from the speaker on her counter. It sounds like Sara Bareilles singing something maudlin about "1000 Times."

Echo likes offbeat music.

"Are you ever going to stop calling me that?" I glare at her. She nicknamed me that at fifteen when I shot straight up, and it stuck. "In case you haven't noticed, I've filled out since then."

I've spent a lot of time in the gym and playing sports to make sure of that.

"Yeah, but you'll always be my string bean…" She sends me a cheesy smile as I follow her inside. The scents of coffee, sugar, cinnamon, and something else delicious I can't put my finger on go straight to my nose and make my mouth water as she lifts a champagne bottle from the nearby counter. "Mimosa? Juice? Beer? Hair of the dog?"

I wince. "No hair of the dog. Jayci and I opened a bottle of gin last night. It was a *bad* idea. She left this morning hung over as hell. I wasn't much better off before coffee." Then I flash Echo a grin. "It was crazy, though. We drunk-fucked on my front porch. I'm pretty sure the neighbors heard."

Pressing her lips in a flat line, she turns for the sink. No snort? No eye roll? No quip? That's not like Echo.

I follow, frowning. "You okay?"

"Fine." She opens the fridge and grabs a bottle of water, shoving it against my chest. "Here."

I take it. "You're not fine. What did I say?"

Echo is quiet for a long moment. "Jayci is nice, but she isn't right for you."

"So? We're just having fun."

Though lately, I've been wondering whether I should try doing something more with my love life than fucking my way through it. It's feeling...stale. But what else is there besides sex?

"Sure. Okay. FYI, it will just be the two of us today."

Our group has been doing Sunday movies and munchies since our early days of high school. Not everyone makes it every weekend, but it's unusual for two-thirds of the group to no-show. "Seriously? I know Kella said last Sunday that she wouldn't be able to make it, but..."

"Graham had to pull a last-minute shift. Maryam texted to say she has the flu and feels like death warmed over. I DoorDashed her some soup. And Xavian..." Echo tucks a stray curl behind her ear and...is she blushing? "Um, he called a bit ago. He's got a paper to finish."

"Professor Akbar's financial theories project, right?" At her nod, I shudder. "I scrambled to finish that sucker last year before graduation. That essay is no joke. And everyone knows what an asshole he is when it comes to grading." Then Echo's words hit me... "Wait. X *called* you?" Not texted. "Like, he dialed your digits and—"

"Talked to me, yeah." She shrugs. "What's the big deal?"

"Nothing." Except it's out of character for my buddy. And Echo is acting...flustered. "I didn't know you and X were that close." The kind of close that would warrant his extra effort.

"Since we both got stuck in that Spanish class with the Russian professor this semester, we've been talking more." Again, Echo doesn't quite meet my stare.

That makes me scowl. "How much more?"

"I don't know. More." She pours herself a mimosa heavy on the champagne and takes a healthy sip. "Want eggs with your French toast?"

I should get to the bottom of this thing with Xavian, but she said the magic words. "You made French toast? For me?"

She nods. "When I figured out the party would be just the two of us, I decided to make your favorite."

"No wonder it smells so good in here." I grab her around the waist and pull her close. "Thanks, shortcake."

"Don't thank me yet. It's my way of buttering you up."

"For what?"

"It's my turn to pick the movie…"

Probably another reason everyone bailed today. The guys usually pick action flicks. Kella likes mysteries and psychological thrillers with the occasional anime film. Maryam chooses blockbusters everyone has seen a hundred times. But Echo is a hopeless romantic. She always picks the mushy movies. And they always make me groan.

Everlasting, til-death-do-us part love is a greeting-card fantasy. Businesses use it as an emotional tool to sell everything from books to flowers to honeymoon destinations. Echo is never going to agree with me, and that's fine. Her eternal optimism is part of her charm. But my family history makes me fairly sure I'm incapable of her notion of love. And I don't know if I can handle ninety minutes of mind-numbing sap this morning.

I grab my phone. "Gosh, would you look at the time? I just remembered that I have a thing this afternoon and—"

"A thing?"

"Yeah, an appointment."

"For what?"

"A haircut."

"You had one last week."

She's right, damn it. I grapple for another plausible answer—and draw a blank. "I mean a doctor's appointment."

"On a Sunday?" she asks dubiously.

"It's a really important appointment. I'm having a lobotomy."

"Right. Well, let's sneak in one last feel-good film before you have half your cynical brain ripped out. It might help you…"

"No, the doctor says I've watched too many of your schmaltzy flicks over the years, so I should see something else before the operation. The more violence, the better."

"You know…" She bustles to the oven and withdraws her famous French toast casserole that nearly brings me to my knees. It's a candy-coated indulgence I don't partake of often, but every time she makes it, I think I've died and gone to heaven. "Maybe you should go home and rest up before your big procedure. I'll eat all this gooey, cinnamony goodness on my own."

It looks amazing, and it smells even better. And damn if Echo doesn't have me right where she wants me. "I could probably move my procedure out long enough to eat that."

"Nope. I'm only serving this during the movie. But it's fine. I'll make it again…someday. Well, maybe I won't. After you've had your lobotomy, you won't appreciate all this yumminess anymore. So I'll probably stop forever. Sad that today is the last time I'll ever bake it, and I made it for you, but…oh, well."

When she drizzles the buttery syrup on top and extracts a plate of crispy, thick-sliced bacon keeping warm in the microwave, I give in. Even the most cloyingly sentimental film is worth the watch if I get to eat that. "All right. You win. Hand me a plate. I'll cancel the lobotomy and stay for the movie."

"I thought you might see things my way." She grins as she hands me a dish.

Despite the dimple in her left cheek, I take it with a growl. "You're punishing me, Hope."

"I'm not, Elliot. After seven weeks of action heroes, twisted relationships, and sophomoric comedies, it's time for something *nice.*"

Echo might have a point. She's the only one who ever introduces movies meant to leave people happy. "All right."

I refill her mimosa while she finishes setting the food on the coffee table in front of the "big screen." The gang makes fun of Echo's TV because it's an old console set from at least twenty years ago. In fact, her whole place is full of half-patched, well-loved hand-me-downs from her older sisters and flea markets. It's nothing like my super-sleek bachelor pad, but I've spent so much time here this place feels like home.

"So what's the name of your torturous flick today?" I ask as I drop to the floor and position myself in front of the table.

Echo is right beside me, bumping elbows and brushing thighs as we settle in. With my next breath, I smell not just our brunch…but that elusive something else sweet that's turning my head and driving me crazy. What is that?

"*Pride and Prejudice.*"

Is she for real? "Didn't I have to read that in, like, tenth-grade English?"

"You had Mrs. Hanover for sophomore lit, right?"

"Yeah." I haven't thought of that woman in years. After the end of that semester, I blocked her out.

"Then you did. It was the best thing we read in class."

"*Lord of the Flies* was way better."

Echo pins me with a withering stare. "You might be a man, but you're such a boy."

"What does that mean? I—"

"Eat, so I can start my movie." She wags her finger at me.

I really would rather not watch this classic chick-flick, even if Kiera Knightly is on the screen. She's hot, despite the billowing dress and any absence of cleavage. But Echo's words bug me.

"Hang on." I shift to face her. "How am I a boy?"

"You don't think much about tomorrow."

"Exactly." I just turned twenty-four. I have the rest of my life to obsess about that shit. I'm not in the market for a wife. After watching my parents, I doubt I ever will be. But I've got a great six-figure job working for an up-and-coming financial services company here in LA. No, it's not Wall Street. I'll be there eventually, once I pay my dues.

Echo sighs. She doesn't like my answer. Funny, we're not together at all…but I hate it when we fight. I hate it even more when I disappoint her. And I clearly have.

"And you just made my point." She shakes her head as she grabs the remote.

"There's no sex in this movie, is there?" I grumble.

"Nope." She rolls her eyes. "Not everything is about sex."

"Sure it is." But she doesn't know that because she's still a virgin at twenty-two. I respect her choice to wait for someone who means something to her, even if I don't share it.

"It's easy to feel your nether regions. Feeling your heart is a lot more complicated. And a lot more significant."

I scowl. Echo almost sounds like… No. She can't possibly speak from experience. Who the hell would she be in love with that I don't know about?

Then I remember she's "talking" with Xavian.

I freeze.

Anyone who called me a player would label Xavian Costa a man whore. She can't have real feelings for him.

Can she?

If I confront Echo head-on about how stupid falling for Xavian is, she'll bristle. So I try to be sneaky. "I haven't talked to X much lately. What's up with him?"

"Besides finals, nothing new. But he's stoked that we'll all be boarding the plane for Maui on Saturday. He was thrilled that, despite being an intern, he was included in the bonus trip for top performers."

Xavian is killing it in the office. He's got a natural gift for making money, so I'm not surprised. But she sounds almost proud of him, like a girlfriend.

"And thanks again for taking me along as your plus one. I'm so excited I bought two new bikinis!"

For Xavian to look at? The thought makes me frown even more. But I act casual.

"Of course. Hey…" I bump shoulders with her. "You're my bestie. I had to give you a graduation trip worth remembering."

"I can't tell you how much I appreciate it. The plane ticket alone must have cost a fortune. But I promise, I won't keep you awake at night snoring." She winks.

"You don't snore, shortcake." I've been camping with her about a million times, so I know. But by now, she's usually found half a dozen activities for us to appreciate the scenery and make memories—a nature reserve, a challenging hike, a sunrise picnic on the beach—something. But we're six days away from the biggest vacation of our lives, and not a word. "Tell me what you have planned for paradise."

"Sun and water!" She closes her eyes and takes in a deep breath, like she can already smell the ocean.

"I meant for us."

Echo turns to me with a shrug. "I thought we'd chill. Besides, I wasn't sure how much you'd have to work."

"I only have two mixers all week. We'll have tons of time for other stuff."

"Oh. Good."

But her voice suggests that isn't good at all. What the hell is up? Does she have some surprise for me and doesn't want me guessing, like Christmas before last?

"So we'll think of some things," I prod her. "Right?"

"Sure."

Her easy reply should make me feel better. Instead, I'm wondering if she's planning to enjoy paradise with someone else.

Like Xavian.

Fuck, I know I've been busy lately and spending a lot of my free time with Jayci—mostly because she'll try anything in bed and could suck the brass off a doorknob—but the thought of Echo and me drifting apart fills me with something like panic.

"What do you say we have a pre-trip graduation party on Friday night? We don't leave until two in the afternoon on Saturday, so—"

"I can't." Echo tears her gaze away. "I've got…something else."

Like? Her vague refusal fills me with dread. "A date?"

"Not exactly."

Shifting closer, I take her chin in my hand. "Then what? Talk to me. Tell me what's bothering you."

"Nothing. I just need to, um…take care of something before we go."

Something? If it's really nothing, why won't she look at me? "I'm getting that you don't want me to pry, but I'm your best friend. Is something wrong? Are your sisters all right?"

"They're fantastic," she assures quickly. "Ella and Carson bought a new house, and they're trying to have a baby."

"Good for them." They seem happy together—at least for now. Hopefully, when Ella has spit out a couple of kids in a few years, Carson won't be tempted by some hot new thing in the office. My dad always was…

"And Eryn is finishing her first semester of college next week. Then she swears she's going to spend the summer redoing the penthouse West bought in Vegas."

"That place was sweet." When Echo asked me to come with her to her middle sister's wedding last fall and we crashed at West's giant-ass bachelor pad at the top of a casino, I never wanted to leave.

But while I'm glad my bestie isn't worried about her older sisters, I'm seriously concerned about her. "Great. Maybe we can visit again when they're done."

"Yeah." She gives me a half-smile. "Sure."

I sigh. "C'mon, shortcake. What's going on Friday night?"

"Just something I need to do." She tries to brighten her smile…but it falls short. "It'll be fine. And once it's done, I'll be ready to spend a week in paradise."

* * * *

"Hey," Xavian calls out to me the next morning as we head for the conference room at the end of the hall with steaming mugs of java.

"I want to talk to you after this meeting," I snarl.

Yeah, I'm in a shitty mood. I didn't sleep much last night. Too much on my mind. Echo's refusal to confide in me chafes. The last time she didn't want to tell me what was bugging her she'd just gotten her first period and was too embarrassed to talk about it. I have no clue what's troubling her now…but I'll bet it has something to do with Xavian.

Does she think she's in love with him?

Yesterday's movie bugged me, too. It was about rethinking preconceived notions of the people you know. Was Echo sending me some message? While the credits were rolling, she tried to talk to me, since we usually discuss the film we've just seen. The movie was better than expected, but I didn't say much else. I was pretty focused on figuring out what she's up to Friday night…and having seconds of her French toast.

Jayci called about nine, wanting a repeat of the previous night. Yeah, she's hot, but I was too preoccupied by Echo and her strangely secretive behavior to have another drunken fuckfest.

And now I'm just annoyed.

Xavian, the good-looking, green-eyed bastard, blinks at me as he takes his seat. "Sure. You all right, man?"

My boss starts the meeting before I can lay into him, so I have a couple of hours to stew. And for my mood to sour. But as soon as the talk about new financial products and market projections are done, I motion to Xavian to follow me to the stairwell. Thankfully, he falls in line, empty coffee cup in hand.

"What's going on?" he asks once we're behind closed doors. "You look pissed."

"What do you have going on with Echo?"

"Nothing." His denial comes too fast. His expression looks too blank.

"Bullshit. She says you two have been talking."

He shrugs. "Some."

Since Xavian never talks to a woman unless he wants something more, I growl. "Why? You'd better not be trying to get with her."

"She's just a friend."

"Then what's with the phone calls? I know you two have something planned this Friday night."

"Shit. She told you?" Xavian frowns.

"She hinted." I stretch the truth a little. Okay, a lot.

"And you guessed the rest..." He sighs. "Look, I was surprised when she asked me instead of you. Maybe it's because you two are so close, and she doesn't want to mess with your friendship? Or maybe she just doesn't see you that way. I don't know. But it will be fine. I've done virgins before. I swear I'll give Echo a good time."

His words buzz in my brain. Echo asked him to take her virginity on Friday night?

What the fuck?

"You agreed to do it?"

"Yeah," he says like it's a no-brainer.

"Seriously? You never do any girl unless she's the hottest in the room. Echo is...Echo."

X rears back. "Dude, what are you talking about? She's smokin'."

Sure, if you like baggy shirts, ankle-length skirts, and clunky footwear. I don't. She's adorable...in her way. She's got a cute face. Admittedly, her eyes are killer. Her outfit yesterday was attention-getting. But overall? I don't see it.

"Besides, I think she'll be an adventurous fuck." He shoots me a sly grin. "I'm looking forward to popping her cherry."

The way he talks about her, like she's just any piece of ass, charges fury through my veins. I lunge at Xavian, teeth gritted. "You will *not* touch her. Ever. Not one finger. Or you will lose them all. Do we understand each other?"

X frowns. "What the hell? I'm not going to hurt her, just give her the 'vitamin D' she asked for."

Fury turns to lava and nearly oozes from my pores. "Echo did *not* ask you for dick."

"Not in those exact words. But...you know. She's finally ready to get laid. Who can blame her?"

I can. She's said for years that she's waiting for someone special to make her first time memorable. Xavian isn't that guy. She should be too smart to fall for his well-used charm. So why did she pick him?

Seriously, is there any way she's in love with him?

"Don't be pissed, dude. Why does it matter?" He cocks his head.

"Are you put out that she didn't choose you?"

Kind of. Yeah. I'm her best friend. No one is closer to her. And she didn't confide in me. She knows I'd do anything in my power to make her happy.

What if she asked you *to take her to bed?*

I don't know.

"What exactly did she say?" I demand.

Maybe X misunderstood. Maybe he heard what he wanted to and ran off with some half-cocked idea. Maybe he's even yanking my chain.

Xavian shrugs. "Just that she'd promised her sisters she'd never let guys or partying derail her education. But by graduation Friday morning, she will have officially kept her word. Then…I don't know. I guess she's curious about sex."

The promise is true enough, but the curiosity? That's not Echo.

Why is she suddenly throwing away her V-card? Is she embarrassed? Is she trying to keep up with Kella, who will proposition any fellow K-Pop, anime-loving metrosexual dude who makes her vagina twitch? Which is great—for Kella. She's happy with variety and never gets attached to any guy she fucks.

Echo isn't built like that. If she got naked with Xavian, she would regret it. And she would cry. I would have to pick up the pieces. Then I would have to kill him.

This has shit show written all over it. I need to stop it.

Luckily, I'm both motivated and devious. "Maybe you're right. It's cool of you to do her a favor and all, but have you thought about…after?"

"No. I've slept with a bunch of girls I still call friends. It's only weird if someone makes it weird."

"Sure. I'm in the same boat with Jayci, Lindsay, and a few others. You're totally right." Except when it comes to my best friend. "But how will Echo be once the deed is done? Look at the movies she picks. *Beauty and the Beast. Fifty First Dates. While You Were Sleeping. Pretty Woman. When Harry Met Sally. Sixteen Candles.* And what does she refuse to watch? *Titanic. The Notebook. Ghost. The Bodyguard. La La Land.* All movies where the two main characters don't end up together. Think about that."

"You saying she'd turn into a clinging vine?"

"Like ivy growing on the sunny side of a house, pal." I clap him on the back with a nod.

Honestly, I have no idea if it's true, but I'm not going to stand by and watch this debacle to find out.

Xavian pales. "I didn't think about that. It will make the whole group weird if she can't separate a favor from death-do-us-part."

"Yep."

"Is that why you've never gone there?"

In all honesty, I never gave hooking up with her a thought. We met as kids. Sure, I noticed when Echo grew boobs and her hips filled out. She's female, and I'm not blind. But she's always just been…there. She's my kind, outdoorsy best friend whom I taught to drive because her workaholic parents were too busy. She's my soft-spoken hippie-chick sidekick who makes the best French toast on the planet—which is why I can forgive her for puking after too much wine, her Boho-chic vibe, and her love of sappy movies. But she wants the sort of happily-ever-after her sisters both seemingly have. I'm no one's forever…but I won't let Xavian rip off her rose-colored glasses.

"More or less," I reply. "And I'd never want to hurt her."

"One hundred percent." X nods like he's rethinking everything. "You're right. I hate to disappoint her, but…"

"I'm telling you, man, what's going to happen if you agree to this." I shrug with a nonchalance I don't feel. "But do what's right for you."

And I'll do what's right for Echo—even if she doesn't know it.

I already have a plan to ensure Xavian is so busy Friday night, he doesn't have two minutes to piss, much less pluck my best friend's V-card.

Echo will be furious if she ever finds out, but I stand by my decision. And I know how to deal with her. Besides, she's always quick to understand and even quicker to forgive. How bad could it be?

Chapter Two

Friday, May 11

The end of the week finally rolls around. Echo texted me yesterday afternoon with the news that she'd finished her last final of college ever. And she got a ninety-four. I congratulated her and offered to take her to dinner at her favorite seafood place to celebrate.

Echo rarely turns down food, and she never says no to Pescada Fresca.

But last night, she did.

Her refusal bugged the shit out of me. It shouldn't have—it's entirely likely she was exhausted after a grueling week of tests—but I spent half the night keyed up and agitated, wondering what the hell is up with her.

I'm still vaguely unsettled as I greet Kella and Graham to watch the last of our matriculating friends officially graduate. Unfortunately, Maryam still isn't over the flu.

The ceremony is a typical commencement—hours of speeches, unfamiliar names, and a sea of single-colored robes—but finally Xavian Costa and Echo Hope walk across the stage and receive their degrees.

We sneak from our seats, get the fuck out of the domed stadium, and meet the others in the parking lot where we share hugs and hearty congratulations. Kella even gets uncharacteristically emotional and sheds tears, so, of course, soft-hearted Echo joins in, her barely glossed lips tremulous as they hug.

Then she makes her way to Graham, pausing to talk. As usual, he says something that makes her laugh.

"Thanks for coming, man." Xavian sticks his hand out to me.

I shake it. "I wouldn't have missed it. Congrats! And next month, you'll start your big-boy job down the hall from me."

He laughs. "Fuck you."

We've been friends since joining the same Scout troop as gawky ten-year-olds. He spent a lot of nights at my house because his single mom worked multiple jobs to keep a roof over their heads. His shitbag father—whoever he was—ran out before Xavian was even born. We're almost as close as brothers.

But all I can think right now is that the motherfucker better have taken a giant step back from Echo.

"So…did you tell her?" I ask in low tones.

"That I've got to work tonight? Yeah."

"What did she say?"

"She understood, but she was disappointed."

That X isn't going to teach her the mattress tango? Fuck. If she has actual feelings for Xavian, I need to quash those before he hurts her.

Should I remind her that, during their senior year of high school, he bet Graham and me a hundred bucks that he could sleep with the entire varsity cheerleading squad—and that we all had to pay up a month before graduation? As a teenager, I tipped my hat to him because I'd taken the same bet the year before and only made my way through half the team. As an adult, the wager sounds stupid and sophomoric. Cringy. But if Xavian took that bet today—and he probably would—he'd succeed again.

Honestly, he's not a bad guy. But he's dead wrong for Echo.

Still, something made her ask the man whore to be her first. What?

"She'll get over it," I murmur to him. "A week in Hawaii will distract her."

Xavian rubs at the back of his neck. "She hinted that we could get to it there."

No. That isn't fucking happening. I'll make that impossible, even if I have to glue myself to her side every moment of every day.

"What did you tell her?"

"I was vague."

"Find someone to do when we get there, huh?"

"Are you kidding? Hot tourists in bikinis who have had too many mai tais? Hell, yeah. But, um…I got a call from a guy named Sakamoto yesterday. He's a PI who seems to think I have long-lost relatives on my dad's side. Apparently, they're interested in me, so I'm going to spend some of my free time looking into that."

"Yeah?" His lack of family has always been a sore spot for Xavian, especially since everyone else in our friend group is loaded with parents, siblings, aunts, uncles, cousins... X doesn't have anyone since his mom died a few years ago. "How do you feel about that?"

"They want a blood test. I guess they're super rich or something. Whatever. If it turns out we're related...we'll see."

I hope my buddy someday gets the kind of family he's always wanted. Maybe then he can brush away that chip on his shoulder. And if this distraction keeps him away from Echo while we're in Hawaii, even better.

From the corner of my eye, I catch Echo pull back from Graham's brotherly embrace. Then her stare falls on me. It's so automatic to hold out my arms and for her to fall into them.

Something good settles into my chest as I hug her. "You did it, shortcake."

She smiles up at me, teary. "I did. I wish Ella and Eryn could be here. My education was only possible because they sacrificed theirs for me."

"I'm sure they wanted to come. But since we're leaving tomorrow, you wouldn't have had much time to spend with them."

"That's why we're planning our great, big sisters' adventure later this summer."

I nod. "So do you feel all accomplished now?"

"Mostly."

But not entirely?

"Hey, I have to get back to work," Graham says with a wave.

Kella follows him. "Me, too. Sorry. Have a great time in Hawaii! We'll have a graduation blow-out when you get back. And Maryam should be over the plague by then."

"Sounds great," I call.

"See ya!" X waves.

Echo smiles and blows them kisses.

Then the three of us are standing alone, Xavian and I both staring at Echo. An awkward silence falls.

"Lunch?" my buddy asks.

Normally, I would say yes—I'm starved—but if I can get him to fuck off, I'll have that chat with Echo I didn't get last night.

"Don't you have a mountain of work to finish before we take off?" I send Xavian a pointed glare.

"Yep. I do. I guess...I'll get to it. We'll party in paradise. See you two at the airport tomorrow."

"'K. See you then." Echo leaves my arms—and walks straight into Xavian's. "I'm proud of us."

He cups her face, and I don't like the way he looks at her. I clear my throat meaningfully.

"Fuck, yeah." He backs away and weirdly high-fives her, breaking the moment. "First in our families to graduate."

Echo laughs. "Right? We need to *really* celebrate next week."

Is that code for *I want to have sex with you?*

"We will." Then I turn to Xavian. "I'll see you at the office, buddy. I'll just be a few minutes."

X takes my not-so-subtle hint. "See you there."

When he's gone, I turn to my bestie. "Need a ride back to your place?"

We can talk there.

Echo unzips her graduation gown and steps out, draping it over her arm. Her dress beneath stops my breath. It's not her usual shapeless, ankle-length sack in earthy brown or mustard, decorated with old-fashioned flowers and floppy ruffles. Nope, this is a rich wine color, trimmed in matching lace that somehow makes her golden skin glow. It's also short. *Really* short. Like, she better hope there's not a stiff wind short. But wow, I've never noticed her tanned legs before. They seem miles long.

"I'm good. I rode my bike."

When she turns to point at the rack, I catch a glimpse of her mostly bare back, minus two straps hugging her shoulder blades and a delicate tassel dangling in between.

Holy shit. Is she trying to attract attention? Granted, it's another hot day, but lately her long skirts and combat boots, braids, beanies, and plaids have been replaced by stuff that's a lot sexier.

I look away because I shouldn't be staring at my best friend like *that*. "Cool. Um, I want to talk to you. Why don't you feel totally accomplished? Your major wasn't easy, but you made amazing grades, despite having to work to help with tuition and pay rent. You have lots of friends, the respect of your professors, tons of prospects…"

"I know. And I'm proud of all that." Then Echo looks away, sinking her slightly crooked front teeth into her puffy pink lip. "I just wanted to make today about my new life. I woke up feeling like the usual me. I'm an adult, but in my head I'm still a kid since I haven't done all the grown-up things like start a career, make car payments, worry about taxes…and other stuff."

Like have sex?

"I wanted to finish the day totally embracing the life I'm going to have. Graduation was a big part of that, for sure. I had a plan to work on some of the other stuff. I even have an interview at three o'clock with a firm I think could be a great fit for me, so I'm excited…" Echo shrugs. "But the rest of my plan fell through. It can wait a few days, I guess."

Yes, she means having sex. Clearly, she's not going to tell me—I have a few theories about why—and I can't confront her with what I know.

I have to tread carefully.

"There's no rush on anything, Echo. You are an adult. It's clear you're a woman and—"

"Is it? Really?" She thrusts a hand on her hip.

I don't think she means to, but her pose shows off her curves and makes it abundantly clear that she's all woman.

Seriously, I have to stop looking at her like *that*.

"Of course. You'll get a good job, I'm sure. You won't be able to avoid taxes, trust me. And car payments are overrated. The more adult decision might be to drive your paid-off clunker a bit longer. Anything else you feel like you're missing out on will come in good time."

"But I've already waited, probably too long because I stupidly want something that will never happen…" Her face closes up, and she shakes her head. "Never mind. Not your problem. I'll figure it out."

What is she saying? That she wishes she'd lost her virginity sooner? That she regrets holding out for a fairy tale?

"Don't give up, huh?" She may not find Prince Charming, but someday she'll meet someone. He'll have to be close to perfect to deserve Echo. And before I let him near her, I'll have to trust that he won't break my best friend's heart. If he does, I'll break every bone in his body. "You got this. I believe in you."

She gives me a wry smile. "I appreciate the vote of confidence, but one of the hallmarks of being an adult is realizing when it's time to be realistic. So I'll reschedule what I'd planned for tonight another time."

Like hell. She had something more meaningful in mind than a one-night stand with Xavian. She's entitled to at least that much, and she shouldn't settle for less. "Echo—"

"It's fine," she assures. "You heading back to the office?"

With a sigh, I glance at my phone. Three voice mails, half a dozen texts, and a meeting that starts in under an hour. Fuck. "Yeah. You want to hit Pescada Fresca tonight, just the two of us, to celebrate?"

She flashes me a dismissive smile. "It's really sweet of you, but I've got lots to do. I'll see you tomorrow."

After lifting a hand in a half-hearted wave, she heads to her bike. It takes everything in me not to call her back. But what the hell would I do then, ask if I can help with her "problem"? That would be not merely crossing the friend line; that would be stomping it into dust before I bulldozed what was left of it. Besides, I'm no better for her than Xavian. The difference is, I know it. No clue what he's thinking, but I need to keep those two apart, make sure Echo doesn't do anything she'll ultimately regret, and encourage her not to give up on her dreams.

* * * *

Time drags by until Echo, Xavian, and I meet up at the bar in the airport the next day to wait before we board our flight. I order a vodka cranberry. X starts with a spiked coffee since he was at the office until nearly four this morning finishing up the project I had my boss dump in his lap so he couldn't rub his uglies against Echo last night. Except for another eye-poppingly short skirt, she seems like her usual sunny self again as she orders a piña colada.

"Here's to our adventure in paradise." I hold up my glass.

"Amen, brother." Xavian lifts his mug, then swallows back half of the brew.

"I can't wait!" Echo looks giddy. "My sisters are really jealous. Eryn assures me I'm going to love Maui and that I'm never going to want to come home. She told me to at least do a drive-by of the Sunshine Coast Bed-and-Breakfast where she and West honeymooned."

"Then we will," I promise her. I want to take a drive around the island anyway to see as much of it as I can.

X sucks back the last of his spiked java, then motions for another. "And I should know no later than Wednesday if I have a long-lost family, so we might have that to celebrate soon."

"You submitted a DNA sample?"

"Yeah. Why not? If we're not family, no harm, no foul." He shrugs.

"Do you know anything about them?" Echo asks.

"Nothing except that they're well aware Daddy couldn't keep it in his pants."

"Oh, maybe he and my dad were pals," I quip. "They had that in common."

And given Xavian's track record with women, I wouldn't be surprised if he turns out to be this womanizing bastard's son. After all, the apple doesn't fall far from the tree.

"Right?" X shrugs. "If this pans out, I guess the family will tell me more. Until then, I'm waiting."

"Whatever happens, I hope you're happy with the outcome," Echo murmurs.

"Thanks."

"Hey," I call to her as she sips more of her fruity drink. "How did the interview go?"

"Oh, really good. If I get the job, I'll be working as the social media manager for a nonprofit that helps solicit gently used play equipment and other donations for at-risk kids. It's a little organization and it probably doesn't pay shit." She gives me a self-deprecating grin. "But you know me."

I do. "It's meaningful work that sounds right up your alley."

"Exactly. It won't be like work at all. I think there's a good chance I got the job. Bruce Henderson, the guy who runs the place with his wife, Fay, said an organization like this helped him stay off the streets and out of gangs as a teenager growing up in one of the rougher parts of LA. They're both retired lawyers now, and they're dedicating their lives to making the city a better place."

"That's fantastic." Xavian hugs her before I can.

The second he pulls away, I toss him a glare. How the hell is Echo supposed to stop thinking about having sex with him if he won't stay out of her grill?

X shrugs, then reaches for his second cup of spiked coffee as the bartender slides it his way.

I turn back to Echo, who's peeling off a familiar oversize beige cardigan to reveal a gauzy blue dress that ties around her neck—and a V that plunges to her waist.

My eyes go wide. Echo has cleavage? Yeah, *lots* of it. I knew she had boobs. I just hadn't really looked at them before.

Kind of hard not to now. Her curves are so...curvy, it's hard to look away.

Slam the brakes on that train of thought, buddy. Quick.

"Congratulations," I finally manage, giving her the briefest hug possible. "Will they call you this coming week?"

"Probably. I mean, I'm not taking anything for granted, but they're in a hurry to fill the vacancy left by a woman who just had her second baby and decided to stay home with her kids. And"—she sends me a stilted smile—"I'm hoping it doesn't become an issue, but Fay liked me so much, she tried to persuade me to go out with her son. I didn't want to insult her, but I was eager to end any expectation that I would date where I work, so...I told them you're my boyfriend. Sorry. It happened so fast. I didn't know what else to do."

"That's fine, shortcake. I'll come to your rescue if you need it."

She looks relieved. "Thanks."

"Anytime." I keep my stare pointedly on her face, looking into her golden brown eyes so my gaze can't stray to the soft swells of her breasts spilling from the plunging front of her sundress.

She's got to be wearing all this revealing shit to tempt Xavian. That isn't entirely his fault...but I still want to punch him in the face.

An hour later, I'm relieved to help Echo back into her cardigan before she boards the plane. Seeing so much of what I'm convinced are healthy D-cups has me on edge.

The company bought first-class tickets for X and me, and I refused to make Echo ride back in steerage, so I splurged to grab her the seat next to mine. Xavian is directly behind me. Once we take off, the drinks will flow and the party will be officially underway.

Except when we board, the flight attendant approaches Echo to ask if she'd move to the seat behind her—the one beside Xavian. I tell the woman wearing a blue polyester skirt and an indifferent expression that Echo and I are traveling together. She merely shrugs and says her hands are tied.

Echo sends me a sad, if apologetic, stare, then sinks down next to the guy she begged to take her V-card. Thirty seconds later, a dude in a suit plops in her seat, looking watchful and exacting. If he's not some bigwig with the airline, then I'm not an investment portfolio manager.

The flight drags on forever. I try to watch movies, but I'm keenly aware of X and Echo talking nonstop behind me. I can't hear what they're saying, but she's tossed off her sweater again and leans close to him. And there's her cleavage, which he's not even trying *not* to look at.

I need to stop stealing glances, too. What the fuck is wrong with me?

When we deplane, I stand to watch her slide her Birkenstocks back on, then rise to her feet. One of the spaghetti straps of her dress falls off her shoulder, hanging halfway down her arm. Before I can right it, Xavian trails a finger up her arm slowly, smiling as he settles the thin band back in place…and lingers too long.

"Thanks." She sends him a sunny smile, then turns to me. "How was your flight?"

Too long. It sucked. The suit glared a lot and smelled faintly like sweat. "Fine."

"Ours was really nice."

"It was great," X seconds.

Yeah, because you spent the last six hours ogling her tits.

As she tries to exit her row, my best friend trips on her own two feet. "Oops. I probably shouldn't have had so many glasses of wine."

X laughs as he catches her around the waist—and doesn't let go. "You're giggly."

And you're handsy, asshole.

I help her into the main aisle, warning Xavian with a scowl.

The trip through the terminal is less eventful. Thirty minutes later, we all have luggage, then we trudge outside to find the rental car counter…only to groan at the long line.

"One counter?" Echo sighs.

She's usually really patient. Today, I'm the one soothing her. "It won't take that long, shortcake."

"You're a liar, string bean."

That crooked smile I know so well makes her look not just familiar, but surprisingly pretty as the day's fading rays light up her caramel brown waves and sun-kissed skin.

If I'm thinking about my best friend as a woman, I'm clearly jet-lagged. I focus on the long line.

It takes nearly an hour, but we make it to the counter, secure the convertible I booked for the week, then take off with our luggage, the useless paper map, and our sense of adventure as Cardi B screams "I Like It" over the radio.

The hotel is in Wailea, on the southwest side of the island. A half hour later, the road winds a quiet, lush path down to our resort, Echo points and gasps at nearly every palm and every beautiful vista. I smile. This is why I brought her. I knew she'd love it. And we'll make some awesome memories together. We've been doing that since we started attending the same elementary school. It didn't seem right to come to paradise without her, even though that means I'm giving up sex this week.

Once the valet takes our car, we step into the open-air lobby.

Echo gawks, open-mouthed, at the stunning view of the ocean.

"Fuck…" X mutters almost under his breath.

Yeah, the lush foliage, swaying palms, and profusion of flowers are even more eye-popping than I imagined. It's going to be an awesome week of paradise, booze, parties, and fun.

Check-in is painless, and a sexy AF Hawaiian woman in a bikini top and grass skirt shimmies up to put a lei around each of our necks.

"Aloha." Her gaze lingers on Xavian.

My buddy winks her way. "Aloha, beautiful. Thanks."

She smiles and disappears to greet more incoming guests.

"Can we go straight to the beach?" Echo pleads, still gaping at the shimmering Pacific.

I wrap an arm around her waist and guide her away from the steps leading down to the water. "We've got to drop off the luggage at least. The car rental took longer than expected, so our dinner reservations are in"—I glance at my phone—"forty-five minutes."

"All right," she grumbles.

Reluctantly, she lets me guide her to the next waiting car up. But it's half full of beachgoers wrapped in fluffy resort towels, smelling of salt and dripping water. Echo and I fit inside with our luggage, but there's no space for X.

"I'll catch the next one," he assures us.

"Sorry!" Echo calls as the doors begin to slide closed.

But Xavian isn't bothered. Before I lose sight of him, he's already making small talk with the Hawaiian hottie with the soft hips and ten-out-of-ten tits. I fully expect he'll lay the giver of leis. Which is great because then he won't be trying to lay Echo.

Finally, we make it to our suite, both amazed at our huge balcony with full-frontal views of the ocean. She dumps her luggage in the living room and rushes outside with a gasp.

I follow, feeling the same. "Pictures don't do this place justice."

"At all. Wow…" She turns to me with a huge smile. "I can't believe we're going to spend the week here. Thank you. Seriously."

I bring her close and kiss the top of her head. Since she's wearing her baggy cardigan again, I can almost forget how much cleavage she's got underneath. "You're welcome. I'm going to take a shower before dinner. Unless you want one first."

"A quick one. Five minutes."

"No problem."

We jockey around the fact we only have one bathroom. It's a big one, complete with a sunken tub and plush robes. But we do all right. By the time I step out of the bedroom in clean clothes, Echo turns to me wearing another short dress—this one a rosy shade with a three-tiered skirt that barely reaches mid-thigh. The curvy swells of her breasts are on display again, along with a huge smile. She's done something to her face besides put on a little colored lip gloss. Her eyes seem bigger. Her skin already looks somehow glowing and tan.

I've never seen Echo look more than cute. Right now, she's beautiful.

"Wow, you look great." I've complimented her appearance a hundred times and meant it...except when I tried to be nice because she was sick and looked like hell. This is the first time I've ever felt awkward saying something. Does she know I mean it more than I should?

"You clean up nice, too. Xavian just texted. He'll be a few minutes late. I guess it took him a while to get into his room."

More likely he hung around the lobby with Miss Hawaiian Ta-tas. Does Echo suspect that? Would it upset her?

We head down to the restaurant, and the maître d' sits us beside a short iron railing with gorgeous views of the property and the beach. Five minutes later, we have a cocktail. We clink glasses and order appetizers, then look up to see Xavian rushing to the table in his collared shirt and khaki shorts.

"Sorry, guys." He slicks back still-wet hair and takes a seat. "What did I miss?"

Moments later, the waiter delivers appetizers. X scans the menu while we give our orders, then he tells the smiling older man in the Hawaiian print shirt to bring him some mahi-mahi and a mule.

We make small talk about the resort, work, and school while we consume liquor, food, then more liquor. It's nice, like old times—mostly. I hate that I'm noticing that the exposed flesh of Echo's breasts playing peekaboo with her dress are a few shades lighter than the rest of her.

Is that as pale as her skin gets...or are there other parts of her not only unseen by any man, but the sun?

I shouldn't speculate about that. I shouldn't be thinking about her at all. And the way X is looking at Echo, I'm convinced he's wondering the same thing. I want to throttle him.

Glancing down into my greyhound, I swallow to get my temper under control. Despite the fact I've warned X away, he's not backing off.

I'm sure he thinks I'm jealous or something. But I intend to keep my best friend from getting hurt.

Dessert comes. Echo digs into her brown butter banana, dripping in caramel sauce and slathered in ice cream, and she moans. The little sounds from her throat have me pushing my cheesecake away and shifting uncomfortably in my seat. I'm hard just from listening, I admit it. She's sounds like she's having a fucking orgasm.

Has she ever had one?

None of my business. I need to stop wondering shit like that.

A glance tells me Xavian, staring fixedly at Echo, is having dirty thoughts, too.

I motion to the waiter for another drink. X points to his glass, as well.

Fuck, maybe it was a mistake to think I could sleep in the same bed with my best friend, no problem. Something tells me it won't be as much like putting my sleeping bag next to hers as I believed.

Finally, she finishes the last bite of her dessert with another wrenching moan, eyes closed as she licks her spoon like a lover.

Shit. Echo is…sexy? When did that happen?

In front of me, my phone rings. I glance at the display, then smile. "Hey, Gramma."

"How's Hawaii, young man?"

"It's gorgeous. I'm sitting here on the open lanai, finishing dinner and drinks with Xavian and Echo. How are you?"

"I hate Boston, and your grandfather, may he rot in hell, insisted on living in this shit hole. And now I'm too old to leave."

"You're not. If you want, I'll move you to Cali the day I get home. I'd love to have you closer." I worry about her now that she has no family back there to take care of her.

"I'm not pretty enough to live in Hollywood. Besides, you can't move my house, and I'm not leaving it."

We've had this argument before. "Stubborn broad."

"Headstrong ass," she quips back.

I laugh. We've had this argument before, too. She raised me during summers when my mom was working two jobs and my dad was too busy plowing his new piece of ass on "business trips" to be bothered with his kids.

"Hi, Gramma Liddy!" Echo calls across the table.

"Tell that young lady of yours I said hi. And tell her I said to keep you in line."

"Gramma, we've talked about this…"

She's convinced Echo hung the moon and I should marry her tomorrow. It's precisely because I care about her that I never would.

"And I still think you're wrong. You're not your philandering father. He came out of my vagina a raving asshole. Never did care about anyone but himself. You're not like that."

"Thanks, Gramma." What the hell else am I going to say when my grandmother is talking about her female parts while Echo and X look on intently?

"She'd be good for you. Snap her up before someone else does. Life is too short to spend it without the people you love. I found that out again yesterday." She sighs. "Rose died."

Damn. Rose was her best friend for decades. "I'm so sorry, Gramma."

Suddenly, my salty, tough-as-nails grandmother who's outlived both a husband and a worthless son bursts into tears.

Quickly, I mute the call and stand. "Sorry. Charge dinner to the room. I need to talk to Liddy. She's upset." I glance Echo's way. "I'll be upstairs."

Then, with a meaningful glare at Xavian, I leave.

Thirty minutes and a lot of shared memories later, I hang up, hopeful that my grandmother will bounce back to her spicy self soon, and splash some water on my face. I look like shit. I'm jet-lagged, my body thinks it's three a.m., and I'm wondering where the hell X and Echo are. Can they really still be in the restaurant?

As I set the hand towel aside, the latch clicks and the door opens. I head in that direction. "Echo?"

When I round the corner, she looks gutted. Tears spill down her cheeks.

Seeing her hurt is a visceral pain.

"Shortcake, what is it? What's happened?"

If Xavian touched her, I'll kill him. No ifs, ands, or buts.

"You made sure Xavian couldn't spend last night with me?"

X must have spilled. And she sounds crushed. "For your own good. He's a player. I wanted to protect you."

"I didn't ask you to. I wanted to lose my virginity on my terms with someone who knew what he was doing and would make it all right." More tears fall. "Why would you take that from me?"

Is she serious? "Because you deserve more. I know you want that."

"And who's going to give it to me?" She looks me up and down. "You?"

Since she's slung her ugly cardigan carelessly over her arm again, flashing cleavage, it's easier for me to imagine being her first than I'd like. "Shortcake…"

"Don't call me that. I'm not a little girl anymore. But you keep treating me like I am. You mean well, but I'm a woman." She tosses her sweater on the nearby chair, storms across the room to me, and grabs my face in her hands. "Damn you."

Then Echo stands on her tiptoes and yanks my mouth down to hers.

Her kiss is graceless and angry…but it's impossible not to notice how soft her lips are and how perfectly they mold to mine.

Lightning zips down my spine as she opens her mouth and nudges my lips apart. I'm frozen and shocked beyond rational thought. Why else would I let her tongue in my mouth? And why else am I closing my eyes, grabbing her dress in my fists while my tongue surges inside, and kissing her like my life depends on it?

Then, holy shit…tingles. Everywhere. Head-to-toe. They spread through my body. Fire follows, razing across my skin and scorching my veins. And that something mysterious I smelled last Sunday at her place above the delectable scent of the French toast? That's Echo. She fills my nostrils again. Her skin. Her body. She's igniting my blood.

Son of a bitch. I'm harder than hard. What the hell is happening?

Your best friend is blowing your mind.

Suddenly, she wrenches free with a gasp, pressing a hand to her swollen mouth and staring at me in horror. "I'm sorry! I'm so… Oh, my god."

Before I can stop her, Echo turns and runs out of our room, slamming the door behind her.

Chapter Three

I stand in the middle of our hotel room, blinking. What just happened?

Echo kissed me. Like a lover.

It blew away every notion I had about her. About us.

Heaving a breath, I stumble back to the bed and sink down. Now what do I do…especially about the fact I'm aching to kiss her again?

The better question is, what happens if you do…and you turn out exactly like your father? You'll break her heart, and you won't have a best friend anymore.

That can't happen.

But she's out there alone, probably confused. She kissed me to demonstrate how ridiculous the notion of us in bed together is…but instead she proved we have blow-the-top-off-my-head, make-my-cock-bust-out-my-zipper chemistry.

I said it before, but it bears repeating. Holy shit.

My first instinct is to charge after her. Then my brain kicks in. If I drag her back to our room now, I doubt there will be much talking. Before I see her, I have to cool down. I have to think without my body throbbing.

Sitting isn't working. I stand. I pace. But no, my lips still burn. My heart pounds. My blood sears me as it races to my cock.

It would be easy to take her sweetness, but she wants things I can't give her. Love. Devotion. Forever.

But Xavian wasn't going to give her those things, either. He hasn't suddenly decided he's head-over-heels with her in the last week. So why did she choose him?

I need to know. And before I find Echo and figure out how we proceed given the fact I can still taste her lips against mine, I have to find out what X is really thinking.

Where the fuck do you think she went? She's not hanging out at the bar by herself with a tear-stained face…

Oh, shit. What if she's already in Xavian's bed? What if she's fucking him?

With a curse, I grab my key from the nightstand, then dash out my door. X's room is just down the hall. I don't see a light on under the door. He's got to be roaming the hotel grounds since nothing else is within walking distance.

Then I hear a woman moan. Not like she's upset or hurt. But like she's halfway to orgasm.

Seriously, X already has her naked and aroused? Is he inside her, too?

Rage takes over.

I bang my fist against his door. "Open up, you son of a bitch. Right now!"

Nothing—at first. Finally, I hear whispers, then scrambling. A light comes on. Then X inches the door open, wearing a pair of hastily donned basketball shorts and a layer of sweat. "What the fuck, dude?"

"You tell me." This is one time I'm happier to be bigger and taller than my pal. I reach over his head and shove the door wide, slamming it against the wall while I charge inside. "I told you not to touch Echo, and what did you do?"

But it's not my bestie sitting on the rumpled bed, holding the sheet up to her flushed, naked body. Just like I predicted earlier when X first got lei'd, he's now getting laid again.

"Shit. I'm sorry." I look away from her, feeling ridiculous. Echo isn't the kind of girl to go straight from kissing me to getting naked with someone else. I need to calm the fuck down.

I'm never a hot-head. I don't like impulsivity. I definitely hate stupidity. Tonight, I've been all of those.

"Happy?" X snaps.

"No, I'm embarrassed. I'm not thinking straight. Echo and I had a fight about last night. She slammed out. I assumed she'd come to you, and when I heard a woman moan…"

"She's missing?"

"No. She's got to be around." Doesn't she? She couldn't take a plane home at midnight.

"But you don't know where she is?"

Admitting the truth sucks, but lying doesn't help. "No."

"Fuck."

"It's fine." I try to convince myself of that. "I'm sure if I look around I'll find her. Don't worry. Um…as you were."

I race out of the room like my ass is on fire and start looking around. There's nowhere in the hallway for her to have gone. There are no lounges or common seating areas on this floor. So I head to the bank of elevators and rush down to the lobby. She's not sitting in any of the plush chairs designed for guests to wait. Like I thought, she's not in the bar. She's not near the taxi stand, which is empty both of cabs and attendants.

Where the fuck did she go? I turn. The sweeping expanse of the moon over the vast blue Pacific gives me an idea.

But when I run down the multiple layers of stairs to the beach, it's empty. All the chaises have been stacked beside a little stand. The sign indicates that check-out for towels and umbrellas will begin tomorrow at eight a.m.

Pushing down my panic, I dash back up the stairs. Where would Echo go when she's upset?

I scan the resort critically. To the left of one of the many swimming pools, I spot a garden area with a sign for a nature walk. And I'm off.

A little bridge leads to a koi pond. Beyond that, a stone path sends me into a lush forest of palms and flowers, subtly lit by the landscape lights and the huge moon. I continue winding down the empty walkway. A sitting area. Another pond. A few discreet information signs about the foliage. Finally, the path ends near a cluster of cabanas around a smaller, adults-only pool that suddenly springs up like an oasis.

There, on the far side, I spot a figure in the fetal position silhouetted against the moon. Her hair and her curves tell me that's Echo.

I bite back the urge to call her name. I don't want to wake anyone, but I especially won't risk her running away.

What the hell are you going to say?

No clue.

Cautiously, I approach the blue-draped cabana and kneel beside her. Tears stain her face. Her mascara runs. Her eyes look lost and confused.

That expression rips at me.

She sits up, blinking and flinching like she thinks I'm going to berate her.

"Hey." I brush a curl from her cheek and tuck it behind her ear. "Let's talk."

Echo looks down before her gaze bounces back up with a too-bright smile. "I'll make this quick and painless. I messed up and I'm really sorry. I was drinking all day and I did more of it at dinner. It was stupid and irresponsible. I said and did things I shouldn't have. I'll be sober the rest of the week and go back to being your only slightly crazy friend."

She wasn't trashed, and that isn't why she kissed me. But confronting her won't help. "I'm not mad. I'm not blaming you, either. You don't need to apologize or spend the rest of the week punishing yourself. But I think we should discuss the reason you plan to lose your virginity and why you picked Xavian." Because I'm definitely not ready to dissect our kiss. "We both know he and his wandering dick will make you miserable."

"I'd rather not talk about it. Can you give me some time alone?"

So she can feel guiltier? So she can put more distance between us?

On the other hand, when Echo is upset she often wants to think alone. What kind of friend would I be if I refused to give her space when she needs it?

Besides, wouldn't it be better for your sanity if she wasn't so close?

"Why don't you go to the room? Text me when you're ready, and I'll come up. We'll talk then, if you want."

She shakes her head. "You go. I'm going to stay here a bit longer."

I'd rather she didn't, but I can't dictate to her. "You have your key?"

"In my pocket."

"All right." With a sigh, I stand.

She sends me a bland, thoroughly fake smile. "I'll see you in a bit."

Then she lies back, turning away from me.

She's shutting me out. That bothers me—a lot. I force myself to walk away, but I can't leave her alone and upset.

On the far edge of the pool, butting up against the garden, is a seating area. I slip into the shadows and sink into the chair in the darkest corner. I wait. And I watch.

She curls into the fetal position again. Her shoulders shake. And I feel fucking helpless, watching her misery. What makes everything worse is, I'm not totally sure why she's so upset. She knows I'm not mad.

Maybe she realizes what you knew the instant she put her mouth on yours.

That kiss changed everything.

It doesn't have to, does it?

Seriously? When was the last time you felt a pull half that strong to any woman?

Never.

Fuck. We're friends. Just friends. Best friends. And it's been awesome. She's honestly one of the most important people in my life. Why would I risk fucking that up when my father's cheating gene makes up half my DNA?

Or is Gramma Liddy right, that I'm nothing like him?

My thoughts turn in circles. I drift off, then start awake suddenly. I'm not sure how much time has passed, but the dark is inkier now. The moon is brighter. Even the random people I heard sloshing in the hot tub on the other side of the hedges earlier are gone. Except for the distant crashing of waves, the grounds are silent.

Thankfully, Echo is still huddled in the cabana. She's sprawled out on her stomach now, using her arm as a pillow, fast asleep.

Yeah, it's probably not a good idea to share a bed with her tonight, but I won't leave her here. And we both need rest.

Slowly, I approach Echo, roll her to the edge of the padded dais, then I lift her against my chest. She curls closer to me, her head nestling trustingly against my shoulder.

That does something to me.

Fuck, this night has been long and confusing.

Slowly, I carry her up the stairs and back to the lobby. One of the cleaning crew darts ahead of me to call the elevator. I thank him with a nod, then head into the car. Two minutes later, I reach our door. Xavian is coming up the other side of the hall.

"You found her. Thank God. What happened?" he whispers, glancing at Echo with concern. "Is she all right?"

"Long story." And I don't really want to tell him. What happened between Echo and me is our secret. If she wants him to know, fine. But I'm not spilling. "Can you reach in my pocket and swipe the key?"

"Sure." He does, then he opens the door.

"Thanks."

He follows me inside, rushing to the bed to yank back the blankets. On soft sheets, I lay Echo down and cover her. She stirs, then rolls to her stomach again, out cold.

She sleeps like that, trustingly exposing her back to the world like she doesn't have a care. But the furrow that settles between her brows, even in slumber, tells me she's still unsettled.

Because she didn't like the kiss? Or because she liked it too much?

Shaking off the question, I cover her, then motion him into the adjoining sitting room, closing the bedroom door behind me. "Look, you said you were going to back away from Echo. Fucking do it."

He shakes his head. "She and I talked again, and I've been giving it more thought. E asked me for a favor. I don't have any reason to say no. I hear you about her possibly getting attached, but she seems clear that it's a completely unromantic arrangement. And I'd rather take the chance that she changes her mind than have her hit up some other asshole who either doesn't care about her or bumbles his way through sex."

X has valid points, but… "I don't understand why she's suddenly so insistent about tossing away her V-card."

My friend shrugs. "None of my business. She asked me to help out. As a friend, I said yes. I don't see the problem. But if you want to dig for her motive, go for it. I'm going back to bed."

"Alone?"

Xavian scoffs like I've got to be kidding. So he's going to nail Ms. Hawaii again before he nails Echo?

Over my dead body.

* * * *

Sleep was a long time coming.

After Xavian took off, I stripped down to my boxers and settled next to Echo in bed. Well, first I cursed a blue streak at my pal for going back on his promise not to touch her, then I slid onto the mattress. The king-size bed should have been plenty big for us both. Not with her so close. I tried to drift off, but Echo's scent was in every breath I took. Her body filled my stare, especially where her short skirt lay precariously, barely covering her ass and exposing a hint of her thin lace panties.

With a groan, I turned away, hard as fuck.

No way was I masturbating in the shower to thoughts of my best friend. So I tossed and turned, finally dropping off around five a.m.

Prying my eyes open now, I stare at the clock. Quarter after noon? I jerk upright. How the hell did I sleep so late?

The other side of the bed is empty. The sheets are cold. Echo has been gone for hours.

Fuck. I scramble for my phone.

Where are you? I text.

The message goes unread.

Lying here won't help me find her—or get the answers to my burning questions. Did she sleep? Is she still upset? What is she thinking? What is she doing?

After charging out of bed, I rake a brush across my teeth and my fingers through my hair, throw on the first pair of shorts and tank I find in my suitcase, then grab my phone—texting Xavian as I leave the room.

Seen Echo this morning?

No reply.

Goddamn it. I hope like hell she hasn't done something rash.

In the hallway, I see Xavian's door propped open by the housekeeper. When I poke my head in, the maid is making his bed and tidying his room. No sign of X.

No matter how many times I press the button to call the elevator, it doesn't come faster. Finally, I reach the lobby and bound down the stairs, scanning the pools on either side of me. Honeymooners? Check. Parents with little ones? Those, too. Teenagers hang out, and retirees look damn glad their days of keeping up with kids are over.

But I don't see either X or Echo.

Retracing the garden path I trekked last night, I search the adults-only pool. But it's so well hidden, the sucker is virtually empty. A senior citizen in a swim cap glares, silently warning me not to interfere with his laps.

Crossing back to the expansive lawn, I scan every visible inch of the property, including the balconies where brunchgoers are feasting. Nothing.

Next, I scramble to the walkway and down the steps, avoiding a screaming passel of kids and a pair of lovers holding hands while eye-fucking. Past a riot of tropical flowers, I reach the end of the cement path and zip my stare over the resort guests hanging out at the hotel's private beach to the soundtrack of someone's too loud radio blasting Nelly's "Hot in Herre."

No sloppy bun or ugly yellow one-piece, which is all Echo has ever worn since her swim team days in the tenth grade. Maybe she's in the water. Maybe she's avoiding me. Or maybe she's with Xavian, who's "comforting" her.

He fucking better not be.

Then a woman's ass in a two-sizes-too-small orange bikini snags my attention. This isn't just any ass. Holy Kim-Kardashian booty. Every golden inch of it is wide and round and juicy perched below a teeny, tiny waist. I shouldn't be distracted when I'm looking for Echo, but this might be the most epic backside I've ever laid eyes on. I'd like to lay a lot more than my eyes on it. She's also got curvy thighs that make me want to run my tongue down one side before I settle my mouth between them.

A glance warns me I'm not the only guy fixated on her long, loose braid swinging from one lush hip to the other, swishing against her pert ass with every slow, barefoot step she takes across the warm sand.

Wait. She moves like… Holy shit. No. That can't be. But this woman is the right height. She has the same shade of caramel brown hair. I know Echo said she'd bought some bikinis…but that can't be the body she's been hiding under ankle-length skirts, too-big shirts, and comfortable sandals.

Right?

Xavian pops up from the ocean and starts chasing her. A giggle sounds above a crashing wave, and before the woman even turns her head, the sinking feeling in the pit of my stomach warns me that the bikini babe with the most fuckable, bootylicious ass I've ever seen is my best friend.

She looks over her shoulder at X with a grin, then tosses her head back when he wraps his arms around her and tickles her ribs.

Yep. It's Echo. Fuck.

And just like Nelly says, it's getting hot up in this joint. Holy shit.

I slept beside *her* last night? Without once touching her? Yep. And I've somehow looked past her without actually seeing her for years.

She turns a mock glare at Xavian before laughing again and poking him in the abs. He retaliates by lifting her into his arms and heading straight for the surf. She squirms and protests. He murmurs something, his green eyes glued to her, his face way too close.

I see red.

"Echo!"

Xavian whips the two of them around. Her smile melts in to a guilty expression as he sets her on her feet. Then I get a good look at the rest of her.

What's left of my composure disappears.

Never mind the cleavage her new and much briefer dresses have been flashing me. This bikini top is nothing more than two nanoscopic triangles, held together by a flimsy string. The swells of her breasts and a mind-boggling amount of side-boob fill my vision. The thin, damp fabric clings. Her hard nipples jut. Water drips down her sun-kissed ribs, licking over the ripe curve of her hips like a lover. I feel an instant, blinding urge to wrap my palms around them and clutch them tight as I sink my cock inside her, hold myself deep, and ruin her for every other man.

Stop thinking like that about your best friend.

But why be less than honest? The desire to strip off that bikini and coax her under me is blinding. Shocking. And undeniable.

"Hayes," she manages finally. "We were just, um…hanging out until you woke up."

Slowly, I close the distance between us. I don't mean to stare, but I can't tear my gaze from her. *This* is the funny, tender, romantic goofball I've been sharing movies, special occasions, and my deepest thoughts with?

How did I not *see* Echo?

And now that I have, I can't unsee her.

I swallow. "You okay?"

A blip of embarrassment tells me she knows I'm asking about last night. "Yeah. You seemed dead to the world when I woke up just after nine, so I let you sleep. X and I had some breakfast and we came out here to catch rays. Want to, um, join us?"

Her voice says she's hesitant to invite me. Because she's still upset about last night? Or because she's noticed the hungry way I'm looking at her?

I have to get my shit together so we can talk, but I don't know what to say. Everything between us has been a mess since we arrived. I promised her a good time in paradise. That won't be in Xavian's bed, so I have to keep her busy and make sure she finds other ways to enjoy her week on Maui.

"Dude?" X nudges my shoulder, then head-bobs Echo's way.

She asked me a question. Right. "Sure. Thanks."

A trembling smile curls up her lips. "Come on. Let's find an extra chaise."

They lead me to a pair of lounges, each claimed by a beach towel, Xavian's snorkeling gear, and the gauzy dress Echo wore to dinner last night.

Xavian confiscates an empty chaise and drags it closer to them, then grabs his gear and heads for the water. "Guys have been hitting on E all morning, and I didn't want to leave her alone to check out the fish. But now you're here. I'll be back."

And…what? Obviously, I won't let another guy approach her. I'll tear the head off the first dude who tries. But with Echo wearing those three teeny scraps of fabric that barely cover the essentials, how does X think I'll be able to resist her myself?

I have to. Echo is my friend, and she's not the sort to come with benefits.

"You okay?" I ask once we're alone.

She bites her lip. Her smile says she's soldiering on. I try not to let my gaze stray below her chin. I definitely don't let myself stare at her more-than-a-handful breasts.

But it doesn't matter. They're burned into my retinas.

"I'm fine. I made too much out of last night. I was tired and worried and a little intoxicated. I really am sorry. It won't happen again." She holds up her arms and tries to grin. "See? Hands to myself."

"Don't keep apologizing." Especially because my less-than-platonic thoughts make me feel like an asshole. "Like I told you, I'm not mad."

"But what I did… It was over the line and—"

"Stop worrying about it and have fun." If she can forget how incendiary our kiss was and go back to normal, I need to try to do the same.

She sends me a grateful smile. "Sure."

We take a quick jaunt into the not-quite-warm water. It's easier to forget how much her bikini doesn't cover when she's submerged, but when she rises from the ocean like a goddess…I watch a droplet run from her collarbones, then disappear into her tiny top, and swallow.

I have to hide in the water until I get control of my embarrassingly unruly cock.

Then a crashing wave sneaks up behind her and knocks her over. Quickly, I swim over to help her up. "You okay, shortcake?"

Echo nods, teeth chattering as she crosses her arms over her chest, making her breasts nearly bulge from her top. "Just a little colder than I thought. The sun will warm me up. I'm going to lay out."

"I'll come with you." Maybe I can close my eyes and pretend she's wearing one of her usual sacks with granny flowers.

As we trek up the beach, I catch sight of a couple eating sandwiches, and my stomach starts to rumble.

"Mind telling me where you found those?" I ask as we pass.

Unfortunately, the guy points up beyond the pool closest to the hotel, and I can just make out a tiki-style stand the resort set up for hungry guests. "It's good, but the line is long. Be prepared."

Even though we should be an hour or two past the lunch rush, he's right. "Thanks."

"Go ahead," Echo says as soon as we reach our chaises.

I don't want to leave her here alone, so I scan the beach for Xavian. No sign of him.

"It'll wait."

She frowns. "Don't be silly. You're hungry. I'll just chill on my lounger and catch some sun. I'll be here when you get back."

My stomach rumbles again. "You sure?"

"Totally." She settles onto her back and closes her eyes, seemingly unaware of the water drops caressing her as they make love to her golden skin.

My mouth goes dry.

"Want anything?"

"Bottle of water."

"Sure. I'll be back." But I can't find the will to leave. I gape. I can't keep my fucking stare off her.

I'm getting hard again. And if she opens her eyes, there's no way she won't see that.

Stop being a lech.

She cracks an eye open. "Something wrong?"

"Nope. I'm, um…making sure I've got my room key."

And now you're a liar, too?

With a sigh, I look around for Xavian one more time. He's nowhere. I sigh.

The hike up to the stand takes forever. Darting around playing kids and resort employees delivering drinks poolside isn't easy. And like the thirty-something guy on the beach warned, the line is long. Thankfully, it moves. And fifteen minutes later, I have a turkey on wheat with swiss and spinach, along with a bag of chips and two bottles of water.

Juggling the food, I trudge back to the beach. As soon as I hit the sand, I glance toward my bestie. But I can't see her anymore. She's been swallowed up by a wall of testosterone.

Are you fucking kidding me?

At least a half dozen guys crowd around Echo, all gawking and drooling, trying to chat her up.

Xavian wasn't lying when he said he couldn't leave her alone on the beach.

Wearing that bikini, what did you expect?

"C'mon, baby. What's your name?" calls one.

Another curls his hand along the side of the lounger, hovering too close. "How long are you here?"

A guy eye-fucking her creeps in. "Did you come with anyone?"

That's my cue.

"She came with me. Get lost." I wedge in between a hulk who's the size of a pro football player and a dude who's got the surfer-bro thing down, complete with a long-bang flip.

Echo sits up as I lower myself to the chaise beside hers. "Here's your water…sweetheart."

She flashes her dimple at me as she takes the bottle from my hand. "Thanks…babe."

With a chorus of groans and grumbles, her horde of boy-toy wannabes wander away.

"Holy shit," I mutter once we're alone. "I wasn't gone twenty minutes."

With a shrug, she perches a pair of round, wire-rimmed sunglasses on her nose and stares at me over the top. "About thirty seconds after you left they started coming over. Xavian shooed them away once. I don't know what they want."

Can she seriously put on that bikini, look in a mirror, and still say that with a straight face?

Maybe she doesn't understand. Has she been wearing her baggy-saggies and flown under the radar of every guy on campus—me included—for so long that she doesn't realize how sexy she is? It's a shock to me, so maybe it's even a shock to her.

"They want you."

She frowns. "Not sure why, but whatever. So what did you get?"

"Turkey and swiss." I take a bite, and we talk about dinner, the honeymoon couple a few loungers down who are getting awfully serious with their PDA for a semi-public beach, and the sublime Hawaiian weather.

After I'm done eating, I spray on some sunscreen Echo brought in her oversize beach bag, then ease back to my chaise. At least since I've returned, the dudes have backed off from my bestie. But I still see them staring. I wish they would fuck off.

But they won't. Neither will Xavian; he's made that clear. And Echo seems determined to lose her virginity this week. Hell, if I hadn't intervened, she would have already spent a night in X's bed…and probably regretted it. She didn't ask me to save her from herself, but shouldn't a good friend do that?

Hell yeah.

But where does that leave me?

Making hard decisions.

Everything boils down to this: Who should be Echo's first, Xavian? Some other asshole? Or me?

Chapter Four

I glance at the clock. Three a.m.

I lie in bed, acutely aware of Echo beside me in a matching pajama set. The sage green shorts with white polka dots cling to her hips and barely reach her thighs. Half of her incredible ass is hanging out. She can't possibly be wearing underwear.

And the tank top… I grit my teeth. It ought to be illegal. It tries to be cute with THE SNUGGLE IS REAL emblazoned across the front. But the spaghetti straps cling by a thread to her otherwise bare shoulders. And the top either shrank in the wash or she bought it too small because it doesn't cover her midriff and it totally grips her tits, emphasizing the fact she's braless.

Everything she's worn this week has made me realize I know Echo as a human—probably better than anyone else—but I barely know her as a woman.

Worse, the question I asked myself on the beach pelts me over and over, circling like a fighter jet ready to drop more bombs on my brain. Do I want to risk her first time being with someone, who, I hope, won't bruise her tender heart? If I did the job myself, I wouldn't worry about her well-being. Hell, I'd worship her—happily. But if I take her to bed— even once—can we go back to being just friends? Would she hate me when I go on with my life?

Maybe. But it's also possible I've underestimated her. Xavian swears she's ready for a one-night fling simply to pop her cherry.

But what about you? Are you *ready to spend a night inside Echo, touching her in every way, then let her go?*

Given how much I want her? The way our kiss last night replays on a constant loop in my head? How hard I am every moment I'm around her?

I don't know.

Suddenly, I wake up to a face full of sun, sweating and disoriented, and glance at the clock again. Crap, it's after ten.

And I hear Echo singing in the shower, bless her off-key heart.

On the nightstand, her phone buzzes.

Glowering, I grab it. If that's Xavian trying to chat her up and into bed, he can go fuck himself. But the display says it's Fay Henderson, co-founder of the nonprofit Echo interviewed with last week.

Shit. She won't want to miss this call, but she won't be out of the shower in time. I hesitate, but on the third ring, I give into the urge to answer. "Hello?"

"May I speak to Echo Hope?"

"She's not here at the moment. This is her…boyfriend. Can I help you?"

"How nice to talk to you, Hayes. Echo told us so much about you. It's obvious she loves you."

Obvious how? "My girl is incredibly special. I'm lucky."

"You are. I was hoping to speak to her. Do you know when she'll be available?"

My gut tells me the woman is going to offer Echo a job. "Half an hour? I can have her call you."

"Perfect. She said you two are on vacation this week?"

"We're in Maui."

Fay sighs. "Bruce and I have been there a few times. Isn't it wonderful?"

We talk for a few minutes about what the older couple did on their last trip to the island, and she gives me some tips about great restaurants and nearby activities.

"I appreciate this," I say, setting the pen beside the full notepad. "Echo would love a hiking tour of Hana."

"It's worth every sore muscle." The woman hesitates. "When you two get back, Bruce and I would be delighted if you'd join us and our son, Brooks, for dinner. We're a small, family-oriented organization, and we like to get to know both our employees and our volunteers. Oops, I shouldn't have said anything, but I guess it's obvious we'd like to offer her a position in our organization."

Echo wasn't kidding. Her prospective bosses are really friendly…and they seem inclined to include their son. In case Echo changes her mind about dating the guy once she meets him? She and I need to look like a couple in love to bear an evening of their scrutiny.

"But, oh... I'm probably getting ahead of myself. Echo hasn't accepted our offer. I really hope she does."

I'm pretty sure she will, but... "I can't speak for her, but I'll have her call you as soon as she's free so you ladies can work out the details."

"Thank you. Enjoy the rest of your week."

Fay disconnects the call. As I set Echo's phone back on the nightstand, she emerges from the bathroom in a cloud of steam with a towel wrapped around her head, barely covered in a thin white nightie that skims her thighs and clings to her curves.

It's so sheer, I can almost see through it.

My mouth goes dry. My cock gets hard.

I turn away before she notices, pretending to rifle through my suitcase. But breathing is a struggle, and I'd be a lying bastard if I said I didn't want to stare more.

"Were you talking to someone?" she asks, crossing the room to pick up her phone.

"Fay Henderson," I tell her, forcing myself not to look at any part of her above her feet.

"She called?" Echo squeaks.

"She wants to offer you a job."

"Really?" Her feet glide across the carpet and stop inches from me.

"Yeah." I pluck a T-shirt and some shorts from my suitcase. They don't match, and I don't care. I need to escape to the bathroom and shut the door between us before I look through her nightgown again...and my will to keep my hands to myself evaporates. "Be right back."

But before I can make it to safety, Echo stops me with a touch. "Wait. You're sure?"

Her voice tugs at the soft spot I've had for her since we were kids. I need to reassure her. Echo's big golden eyes are so wide and earnest. Her rosy lips part. I can't stop thinking of them under mine. Her tits brush my chest.

I don't dare move any closer. In fact, if I don't get the fuck away, I'm worried I'll stop caring she's my best friend, and I'll do something to irrevocably cross the line.

"Positive. Call her. She's excited to talk to you." Then I wrench away, covering my erection with my clothes, and slam the bathroom door between us.

I start the shower. Not twenty-four hours ago, I was too noble to jack off to thoughts of Echo. I'm not too proud this morning.

But my few minutes of meaningless, one-handed pleasure barely takes off my edge. As soon as I end the shower, I hear Echo squeeing and sighing.

I'm suddenly hard again.

We've been friends for most of my life, and suddenly I can't stop seeing her as something more. How much longer can I go on like this? I've been aware of her as a woman for a handful of hours, and it feels like an eternity. How will I last months—or years—wanting Echo and always having her near me but not *with* me?

I don't know, but I need to figure some shit out. She's looking to lose her virginity right now. I either have to let her go with someone else or man up…and deal with the fallout later.

And if it turns out you're an asshole like your father, she'll always regret you.

I've got to distract her until she finds the right man…somehow.

"Hayes," she calls through the door. "I got the job!"

"Congratulations, shortcake." I toss on my clothes and grab my toothbrush.

"The starting salary is better than I expected, and she's so sweet. I hate lying to her…but I don't want to date her son. Thanks for agreeing to do dinner with them. It should only be once. Does the Sunday we get back work for you?"

Not really, since I'll have to touch her, kiss her, act like I love her…and somehow not jump on her. "Sure."

"Yay! We have to celebrate!"

Two minutes later, my mouth feels minty fresh. After tousling my hair with some product, I open the door, praying Echo is dressed.

She's not.

Instead, she unwound the towel from her head, and her dripping hair has slowly wet her nightgown. Worse, the sunlight slants through the window, backlighting her body.

I. Can. See. *Everything.*

Holy shit.

Jacking off was a waste of time and energy.

Forcing my gaze out the window, I sort through my options. There aren't many, and they all suck. Then an idea hits me. It's unhinged, and I'm already questioning my sanity. But as long as Echo parades around our room wearing next to nothing, I don't have any.

"Absolutely. We'll celebrate. Why don't you get dressed? We'll grab breakfast, then have some fun. And I'd like to talk to you."

She approaches, head cocked, eyes soft. "About what?"

"I have a proposition."

Echo looks intrigued, but she shrugs. "Sure. Let me finish getting ready."

She disappears into the bathroom, and it's great to breathe again. But I start pacing. Am I really doing this?

What better choice do you have?

As Echo starts the blow dryer, her phone buzzes. I grab it. There's a text from Xavian. **Came out for an early surf and met a girl. Don't worry. I'll still be good to go tonight.**

Fuck. I don't have any choice at all. Time to get sneaky.

The room service menu is full of things I'm sure Echo will enjoy so I order a few, along with a bottle of champagne. Maybe that will make what I'm about to suggest a little easier for her to say yes.

I feel guilty for the subterfuge…but this is for her own good.

As I'm hanging up, she comes out of the bathroom with her hair half dry, curling softly around her shoulders. And somehow, her nightgown is even more transparent. If I had any question at all about the exact shade of her nipples, I don't anymore.

God, I'm dying to get them in my mouth. They're gorgeous.

So is she.

"I forgot my clothes," she says by way of apology, then bends to rummage through her suitcase.

There's no way to avoid the eyeful of her world-class ass. Well, I could be a gentleman, turn around, and not look. I probably should. But I don't move until she plucks up some garments and disappears into the bathroom again.

Am I really going through with this plan? The better question is, will I be able to pull it off?

Twenty minutes later, Echo emerges again in a golden sundress that gathers tightly across her breasts and ties in a bow just beneath them, emphasizing her cleavage. She's tossed her hair into a loose braid, face made up with a dusting of mascara and some lip gloss. And she glows.

I'm a sucker. I'm an idiot. And I'm going to regret what I plan to say, I have no doubt.

The food arrives, and once the server sets up the table, I sign the receipt. Then Echo and I sit.

I'm nervous as hell, but she dives in, gaping at the stack of pancakes and moaning at the plate of fresh fruit.

She pours some juice while I suck down black coffee and gather my nerve. "What did you want to talk about?"

"Are you absolutely set on losing your virginity this week?"

Echo blinks and blushes, but sets her lips in a stubborn line. "I have no reason to wait. And before you give me all the arguments about why Xavian won't make it special and insist I deserve more, I appreciate that. But he'll make it good, and when I finally have the kind of relationship where sex is involved, I'll be confident that I know what I'm doing."

"If you're sure, Fay's call gave me an idea. Hear me out." I take a deep breath. "Since we'll be having dinner with your new bosses—and their single son—on Sunday, and we have to convince them we're a couple…what if I took your virginity instead?"

A little gasp escapes her lips. "Are you serious?"

No, but the lie will help her.

"Why not? We have this room and this bed and…if you're set on doing this, I want to make absolutely sure you're treated well."

Echo is quiet for such a long time, I start to sweat. And I start to doubt. Would she rather have Xavian? That possibility bugs the hell out of me.

Finally, she sets down her fork and bites her lip. "Would you really do it?"

"If you want, yeah."

She'll thank me for being less than honest when she's found the guy she's really in love with and her hymen is still intact.

Slowly, Echo gets to her feet. I stand, too. She holds out her hand. "I'd like that. I know it wasn't easy for you to offer, especially after we fought the other night, but—"

"Stop worrying about that." I take her palm against mine, aware of my heart gonging against my chest like a wild drum. "Let's take this slow, okay? We have all week. There's no rush."

"But not too slow, promise?"

I just smile. Maybe I'm splitting hairs. I can stomach lying to her for her own good, but I won't break my promises. With parents too busy to notice any of their kids, especially the youngest, Echo has had a whole life of those.

"Come here." I tug on her hand.

She tumbles against my body, and her head falls back. Our stares meet. Jesus, I've barely touched her, and my blood burns, jetting fire to my cock. I'm ashamed of how much I want her, but at least every time I touch her, the desire will be authentic.

The bigger problem is, once I start kissing her, the clothes come off, and I show her what passion feels like, can I fucking stop myself from taking her in every way?

"Be sure," I warn.

If she says yes, I'll do my damnedest to ensure she leaves this week still a proud V-card carrying member, but I'll touch her in every other way she'll let me. And with desire scalding me to my bones, I'm going to enjoy every fucking minute.

"I am," she whispers so quickly, it's clear she didn't think twice.

Electricity pings through my body.

"Then this week, you're all mine. Xavian and every other guy can fuck off."

"Absolutely," she murmurs.

"Good. Are you done with breakfast?"

"Yeah." She skates her palm up my chest, looking at me with pleading eyes. They're impossible to resist. "Are you going to kiss me now? For real?"

She thinks that kiss I laid on her the other night, the one still spooling through my brain, wasn't genuine?

"Yes, I'm going to kiss you, long and slow and hot."

Swallowing, I cup her nape and tilt her head back as I wrap my other arm around her waist and drag her close. If she didn't know this earlier, there's no escaping the obvious now. I'm hard as hell.

Echo's lips part. Her breathing picks up pace. Color rushes to her cheeks. "Hayes…"

The way she half moans my name, like she's on the edge of pleasure, kicks my desire up another notch. "Yeah, shortcake. Come here."

I'm dying to kiss you.

Finally, I close the distance between us and crush her soft lips under my own. She welcomes me with a gasp and curls her arms around my neck, pressing her body to mine.

Fuck, she's like candy. The first time she kissed me, she took me by surprise. Now? There's no mistaking her flavor. Her sweetness lingers on my tongue, addicting. I sink deeper to get more of it. Her scent fills my nostrils, flaring lust through my body.

I need to get closer.

Echo has been my best friend, but right now she's an offering of silky skin, sugary lips, and eager need. I'm a guy, stupid for a pretty face and a banging body. But she's...more.

I'm naturally guarded, but from the day I met her, she's been dedicated to her friends and her causes with open-hearted zeal. I'd prefer to stay home and alone. But she's enthusiastic about new adventures and good times—and determined to bring me along, making sure I enjoy both. I can be a pushy, caustic, suspicious-as-fuck asshole. But Echo is kind. She always believes the best about others, at least unless they prove her wrong.

But I'm not thinking about her sparkling personality as she wriggles her fingers under my T-shirt, trails them up my abs, and palms my hair-roughened chest. Then she brushes a curious thumb across one of my nipples, making me jolt and hiss.

Fuck, I'm on fire.

Desire forces me deeper into her kiss. I lash her tongue with my own, prowling through her mouth like I own it. Her moan becomes a whimper when I fill my hands with her ass and flatten her against my aching cock.

I half expect her to push me away, tell me I'm taking too much, too fast. But no, she stands on her tiptoes, clawing at me to get closer, then lifts her leg over my hip.

Holy shit. If I'm not careful, my fake promise to take her virginity will turn all too real. Hell, thinking I wasn't getting any action this week, I didn't bring condoms...except one emergency prophylactic stashed in my wallet.

Nope. I'm not using it on her. Impulse isn't dictating what happens between us. I need to keep my head and stay the course.

If I don't, my plan will end in disaster, and our friendship will be toast.

It takes all my willpower to tear my mouth away.

"You okay?" I pant.

"Really good."

Her lips look rosy and slightly swollen. I can't stop staring at them. We should talk—about anything—until I get control of myself.

My brain is on board with that plan, but my cock has other ideas.

Before I can stop myself, I skim my lips over her bare shoulder. "Is this weird?"

"Us?" Echo breathes hard, too. "No. Is it weird to you?"

Not as much as I wish it was. I shake my head. "Tell me things you want from a lover."

"Sex."

"More specific."

She hesitates. "What do you like?"

"It's not about what I like. This is about you."

"But..." She frowns. "Shouldn't it be about us together?"

I nearly disagree before I dial it back. Maybe she's right. Being with her won't be like getting naked with Jayci, Lindsay, or any other woman. Coming at Echo with my knowledge of them won't help. Using my familiarity of her will.

"If you're here to learn, I can safely say you've got kissing down."

"Yeah?" She smiles, flashing me that adorable dimple like she's proud of herself.

"Not that we won't do a lot more of it," I add hastily, because if we abandon that and move on...I'm not sure where I'll stop.

To prove my point, I brush my mouth over hers again. Then again. Then once more, lingering even longer. I taste that something tempting on her lips that lures me into taking more of her. I can't resist parting them and drinking her in once more. Her flavor surrounds me, pulls me deeper, and drowns me.

Echo's breath catches, then she groans into my kiss, leaning closer and gripping my shoulders like she's unsteady without me. I'm hungry to pull her tighter, until there's no space or air between us. I wrap her long braid around my hand and tug until I have her mouth exactly where I want it.

I devour her again.

Jesus, I want our clothes off.

Back down. Or the minute we're naked, you'll be inside her.

Exactly! the devil in me points out.

He needs to shut the hell up.

Ending this kiss is harder than stopping the last one. I'm breathing even choppier.

"Yeah, you're definitely good on the kissing part. Who taught you?"

"Mostly Jimmy Corelli."

The swim team captain? "He had a girlfriend. What was her name?"

Her rosy cheeks turn downright red. "Simone. They're married now. But they split up for a while. He wanted her back, though, and asked me if I'd help make her jealous. He seemed so miserable that I did. We made out in the parking lot after school once or twice."

That sounds like Echo's well-meaning heart. "Did you like him?"

"Not really."

"Was he your first kiss?"

She shakes her head. "One of Eryn's friends, Kiersten, had a twin brother, Kaden."

"I remember him." Quarterback. Popular guy. Player. I frown. "He hit on you?"

Echo shakes her head. "I went with Eryn to their birthday party. Everyone played Seven Minutes in Heaven. Kaden and I got thrown together. Is this really important right now?"

Probably not, but that asshole was three years older than her. If he pressured her for more than a peck... It's old news, but I still want to throttle him. "Is kissing you all he did?"

"That time. It happened again the next year. Then he tried to put his hands down my shirt since I'd grown boobs. I kneed him in the balls."

I smile. "Good. Anything else? I should know your experience level so I can figure out how much I need to teach you."

"Not much. So many girls in high school had boyfriend drama. They were always miserable. It never seemed worth it. Besides, no guys ever seemed interested in me."

They were...but I'd put out the word in junior high that anyone who liked Echo had to come through me. That scared most off. The few with enough balls to challenge me? Well, I was an angry teenager without a father figure or parental boundaries, so I was always happy for a fight. That shut up the rest.

"Thanks for letting me know. It's definitely a good thing we agreed to go slow."

She frowns. "But we're going to do it tonight, right?"

"We have all week, shortcake."

"Shouldn't we be spending it in bed? I mean, that's how I'll learn."

"It's going to come natural. So why don't you let me give you the slow seduction you deserve?"

Echo worries her lip. "That's sweet of you, but I don't see the point."

"You don't now, but..." Shit, I need to think of something—fast. "You will later."

She lifts her face and shocks the hell out of me by skimming her lips up my neck, leaving me shuddering, as she kisses her way across my jaw and makes me weak-kneed. Before I can recover, she nips at my lobe and settles against my ear. "I'd rather have you inside me."

Desire flattens me. Huge. Suffocating. Inexorable. How the hell am I supposed to say no to that?

"Shortcake…"

I'm still grappling for an excuse when someone suddenly starts pounding on the door.

Echo jumps, and I'm half expecting someone on the other side to tell me they're from housekeeping. Instead, the banging again resumes.

Both relieved and pissed, I stride to the door and wrench it open to find Xavian standing there, gripping his phone and looking stunned.

"What's wrong?" I scowl.

He swallows, then looks past me to Echo. She's already halfway across the room, and the second she sees his expression, she holds open her arms.

"What is it?" she asks softly.

He tucks her body against his and wraps his arms around her tightly. I don't like it—at all. Then the reason hits me. I'm not just feeling protective. Holy shit, I'm jealous.

X breathes her in and grips her tighter for another moment before finally letting go to face us both. "I have some news."

Chapter Five

Xavian doesn't look devastated, like he lost his job or his best friend. But whatever he's going to say, it's big.

Both relieved and frustrated at his timing, I gesture to the sofa. "Sit down, man. What's going on?"

Slowly, he sinks onto the nearest cushion. "I just got a call. The blood results are back. The PI is right. These people, whoever they are... We're related. They're my family." He sighs. "It's weird to say that."

After not really having any, I'm sure.

"That's amazing." Echo sits and takes his hand. "You have people who care enough to find you so they can include you."

"Maybe." He doesn't sound convinced. "Since they're being so secretive, it's more likely they're not thrilled I exist and they intend to silence me so I won't blab and tarnish dear old dad's reputation."

"Don't assume the worst. Once they get to know you, they'll welcome you with open arms."

There's Echo's optimism again, but Xavian and I are cut from the same cynical cloth. I know exactly why he's convinced this isn't good news.

"Did the PI tell you anything when he called back?" I ask.

"Almost nothing, except the family knows. Sakamoto said he'll be in touch with more from them soon."

Meaning he'll outline what the family wants from Xavian and how much pressure they're planning to apply to shut him up. That could be anything from a bribe to a threat.

What a shitty situation. X could really use some close-knit family.

After his mom died, he went through a self-destructive phase. Graham, Kella, Maryam, Echo, and I pulled him through, but we're friends. He wants a blood bond. He wants to belong with people for life.

The last thing he needs is proof that relatives who should give a shit about him don't.

"Think positive," Echo suggests. "Put out good vibes. They'll come back to you."

Xavian squeezes her hand. "Thanks. Hey, we have until five before the cocktail mixer. Can we get out of here for a bit? I don't think I can just chill on the beach today without going stir crazy."

Good call. I don't think I can keep my hands to myself, especially if Echo and I stay in our room or she puts on another bikini. "You want to have lunch somewhere on the island, then sightsee a little?"

"That would be nice," Echo agrees.

So we all agree to make an afternoon of it, first traveling north and stopping at several scenic points along the way until we reach Lahaina, where we find a fresh seafood place on the beach. Afterward, we backtrack and head south again.

Before we left my room, I'd tucked away the notes I took during the conversation with Fay Henderson. When I passed the suggestions to Xavian, he and Echo both got fired up to hit a local place with ropes courses and ax throwing. We're all experienced climbers, so we challenge ourselves and tackle the most difficult climbing elements.

I swear I've seen Echo a hundred times in spandex shorts, but usually with some baggy T-shirt that covered everything from her neck to her mid-thighs. Not today. Nope, she's wearing a tight crop top in a siren red that clings to her tits, and my good intentions of watching to make sure she doesn't need help climbing—which she doesn't—quickly devolve into ogling her. I can't resist offering a hand or holding her waist.

More than once, Xavian looks at me, brow raised. I have to tell him that Echo no longer needs his "services." If that's too subtle, I'll use small but threatening words to explain that, if he lays a finger on her, I will cut off his balls and feed them to the fish.

At the end of the hike, it's hard to catch my breath…and I can't merely blame exertion. Echo melts against me, panting as she recovers. I can smell her sweet scent. It sneaks through my nose and seeps into my senses. With that comes the memory of her mouth under mine. And her provocative words.

I'd rather have you inside me.

Just like that, I'm hard again.

But not deflowering her is for her own good. I can stand a few cold showers. I can take myself in hand. It won't be the first time…or the last.

I need to think of something besides Echo. Being fixated on having sex with her when we're supposed to distract Xavian from his worries isn't okay.

Echo passes on the ax throwing, which is probably good for me, too. I'm so focused on her I'd probably end up minus a toe or two. Best of all, X seems better off now that we've given him a change of scenery and activity.

"What do you want to do now?" I ask him as we pull away from the adventure park.

Neither he nor Echo has anything in mind, and we still have hours to kill. So we meander through some kitschy shops and people-watch on the beach before heading back toward Wailea.

"Hey, since we're out, could we stop at the bed-and-breakfast where my sister and West honeymooned? It's not too far, and Eryn said they had an afternoon yoga and hibiscus tea thing that was awesome."

I look at Xavian. He shrugs.

"Sure." I nod. "Start the GPS."

Twenty minutes later, I park beside a big white, island-style house with an expansive lawn that gives way to an unspoiled, unobstructed view of the ocean. Not going to lie; it's sweet. Living here would be no hardship.

Outside, two couples mill around with yoga mats, talking while a redhead with an infant sleeping in a harness strapped to her front bustles around, gathering water bottles for everyone with a smile.

I'm not much for yoga. But Echo darts in their direction, so I rush to catch up. X reluctantly follows.

"Hi," Echo says to the woman, hand outstretched. "Are you Keeley?"

The redhead smiles. "I am. How can I help you? If you're here about a room, I'm sorry. We don't have any vacancies this week."

"I just wanted to meet you. My sister and her husband honeymooned with you. Eryn and West Quaid? They said—"

"Echo!" Keeley squees like she's met her new best friend.

That makes my girl happy. Wait, she's not *my* girl as in my girlfriend. Yes, she's my girl friend, but… This shit is confusing.

"You remembered my name?" Echo sounds amazed.

Keeley nods. "I loved having your sister here and was so sad the day she and her husband left the island. But she texted me a few days ago and said you'd be on Maui this week and that you might stop by for a visit. It's time for yoga or I'd chat more. If you've got an hour, have some tea, then we can visit."

Echo looks back to Xavian and me hopefully. We both shrug. Why not?

"Or you can join the yoga," Keeley offers.

"I'd love to. Eryn said your style of teaching and all the poses with the ocean crashing in the background was great."

"I have to admit, the scenery is awesome." The redhead winks.

"How much do I owe you?"

"Nothing. I'm just happy to have you here." Then she calls into the house. "Eleanor?"

A petite woman with graying hair in a pixie cut that accentuates her elfin features emerges, a smile stretching all the way to her blue eyes. "Do you need something, dear?"

"Can you take Kailani?" Keeley pulls the infant from her carrier, then unstraps it. "It's time to start the class. I think she'll go down in her crib now without a fuss."

"Of course." Eleanor takes the baby. "Oh, Maxon called a minute ago. Your husband said he's almost to Harlow and Noah's place. Griff, Evan, and Bethany are already there, conferring. This development...it's awfully sudden."

"My husband's family," she supplies with a smile, then turns back to the older woman. "They don't need me for this discussion, but Maxon better keep it together."

"Well, my daughter wishes you were there." Eleanor drops her voice. "You know Britta can get drowned out by all the loud voices in this family, and she says everyone showed up with attitude today."

"Britta is my sister-in-law," Keeley tells us before she sighs. "I feared everyone would have different opinions."

What the hell are they talking about? I turn to X with a silent question, but he's tuned out, staring out at the ocean, a million miles away.

Not knowing the identity of the strangers and what they could possibly want is killing him. Maybe I should ask Keeley if she has something stronger than tea.

"If this is a bad time, I can come back," Echo offers.

Keeley takes her hand. "You're fine, sweetie. The rest of the brood has this family stuff under control. Do your friends want to join in the yoga?"

Immediately, I shake my head. "Thanks, but we're good."

Keeley cocks her head, then turns back to Echo. "Is this Hayes?"

How the hell does she know my name?

Echo nods. "Eryn mentioned him, too?"

Keeley sends me a speculative smile, then nods Echo's way. "Oh, she did."

I can only imagine what Echo's middle sister said about me. She's never quite believed that Echo and I are just friends. Lately, she's convinced I'm secretly in love with my best friend.

Are you one hundred percent sure she's wrong?

The question is like a two-by-four to the face, knocking my polite smile right off.

"Don't worry," Keeley assures. "It was all good. What about your other friend?"

Echo reads X just right. "He's having a rough day. I think he'd be happy just taking in your view."

"No problem. You ready to get started?" At Echo's nod, Keeley motions toward the wide lanai attached to the house and overlooking the water. "If you two want to sit, feel free. Eleanor will bring you something to drink."

"Thank you." I head X's way and stare over the Pacific with him. "You okay, man?"

"Yeah. Sorry. This shit just keeps hitting me, you know? There are people out there with my blood who went out of their way to hunt me down. I don't know what the fuck they want." He's fighting anxiety. "I hate getting my hopes up."

"I get it. But they don't know you. If they try to heap shit on you now, it's not personal. It's all them."

"I know. And I don't want to be a pussy about this. But is it so fucking wrong to wish I had some of what you have? And Echo has? What all my friends have? My mom died so soon..."

"I know. And I know we're not family, per se—"

"Fuck that, man. You're my brother." He turns to me, trying hard to hold back, but tears sheen his eyes.

"You're my brother, too." I clap his shoulder.

He pulls me in for a bro-hug full of unspoken words. He needs this moment, so I wait until he's steady. But when I glance across the yard,

Echo stands with her head tossed back and the wind teasing the loose tendrils of her hair. Her arms are wide open to the sun in welcome. Golden light bathes her face.

She really is beautiful.

She reminds me of the other thing I need to say to Xavian. "Listen, Echo and I came to an agreement this morning. I volunteered to, um…pluck her V-card. She agreed to let me."

"Seriously? Are you going to do it?"

"No. I know she spouted off about wanting to truly be an adult and do all the adult things, but you know she's a romantic. She's saved that for someone she's in love with."

"You're right."

"And that's not you, man."

"It's not."

Xavian's easy agreement surprises me. I sigh in relief. "And it's not me, either."

He's quiet for a long time. Finally, he peers at me with a dead-straight stare. "Are you sure about that?"

What is he saying? "Echo and I are friends."

"For a long time. But shit changes."

Shock trips my heart. "Did she tell you something?"

He shrugs. "You and I both know women. We've slept with a fuck ton of them. You ever known one who's as loyal and sweet, who's always there when you need them, who's your cheerleader, confidante, and best friend, if she doesn't have serious feelings for you?"

If we were talking about anyone else, I would agree. But this is big-hearted Echo. "Dude, she's always there for you, too. She's there for everyone in her life."

"Not in the same way."

"Only because she and I have been friends longer," I protest.

But deep down, I wonder if that's really true. Is there any chance he's right? Echo gave up the idea of Xavian taking her virginity the minute I volunteered. She didn't even talk to him first.

What does that say about her feelings?

Shit. I'll have to be careful. I can't cross the line with Echo's body or her heart.

Xavian and I pass the next thirty minutes on the lanai with a tropical boozy concoction and a plate of meringue cookies Eleanor brought us with a smile. I watch Echo, trying to figure out where her head is…and if her friendship is actually deeper.

Finally, the yoga session ends, and she runs over, looking relaxed. She glows with a hint of perspiration and pink color from the sun. I try to ignore the way her top clings to her breasts and the hint of her nipples poking through. It doesn't matter, though. I know they're there, and it's a good thing my shirt is long enough to hide my reaction.

But you'll be alone with her again tonight…

Fuck.

"That was awesome!" Echo doesn't merely smile; she looks really centered and happy.

While I wasn't thrilled to just sit here and watch Xavian stew, I'm satisfied that Echo is content. "You did great, shortcake."

"Thanks." She looks at our glum friend. "You okay, X? I'm sorry about staying if you wanted to go…"

"Nah. I'm just chilling with this view. You're good."

Keeley sways in Echo's direction and helps her to a dressing room where she can freshen up with some cool cloths after the session. They return a few minutes later, and we stand. It's after three. We should probably start heading back to the hotel before the cocktail welcome with our CEO gets underway.

Keeley hugs Echo. "It was so great to meet you. I wish you could have stayed to meet my husband, Maxon. He and West got along fantastically."

"I'm sorry I missed him, too. Eryn had nothing but lovely things to say about how special you two made their honeymoon."

"It was our pleasure. When do you fly back to the mainland?"

"Saturday evening."

"If you're free one night before then, let me know. I'd love to have you and Hayes and your friend—I'm sorry, I didn't catch your name—for dinner." Keeley looks inquiringly at X.

He extends his hand. "Xavian Costa."

Instantly, the color leaves Keeley's face. Her mouth gapes open.

"Is something wrong?" Echo asks.

Keeley recovers quickly, but her smile looks stilted. "Nothing. Um… Can you just wait here two minutes? I need to do something before you go."

No idea why the redhead is acting weird, but Echo is dialed in to whatever is bothering the woman. Xavian has already tuned out.

Echo elbows me, so I nod dutifully. In truth, I want to find out why hearing my buddy's name freaked Keeley out. "Sure."

"Two minutes." She holds up her hands, making sure we stay put. "Promise?"

I nod.

Beside me, Echo smiles reassuringly. "Of course."

Keeley turns and runs, sprinting toward the house. Obviously, the yoga has helped get her post-pregnancy body back in running shape because she's quick.

"Any idea what that's about?" I ask Echo.

She shakes her head. "I hope everything is okay."

It's more like five minutes before Keeley returns, still looking rattled. "Thanks for your patience. Can you spare another ten minutes? I want to tell you a story. It's…important."

The inn owner says the words to all of us, but keeps sending Xavian sideways glances.

Now I'm really curious, and we still have a little time before the cocktail gathering. It's not mandatory, anyway. I could use the face-time to schmooze with the CEO, but… "Sure."

"Thank you." She leads us back to the lanai, and we all find a seat, Echo between Xavian and me. Then Eleanor brings Keeley a big cup of hibiscus iced tea and offers us the same. We decline, and when the older woman disappears inside again, Keeley drags in a steadying breath. "When I met my husband, he and his brother, Griff, hadn't spoken a word to each other in three years. It was awful. Their fight was all pride and anger and assumptions, especially on Griff's part. I still rib him about that. Their younger sister, Harlow, tried to be the neutral go-between, but she was going to school on the mainland and had a life of her own. None of them were close to each other or their parents, who were both horrible human beings. I still marvel that those two monsters produced three wonderful, loving people."

That's all interesting—if a bit personal. I wonder how her husband would feel if he knew his wife was spilling the family tea to three relative strangers. I can't figure out why she's bothering, but she keeps on, so I'm guessing she has a point.

"Harlow's husband is…" Keeley searches for the right words. "Let's just say Noah knows a lot of people. He was in the airport one day when a stranger approached him. The man said he thought he was Harlow's long-lost brother. After a little digging, that turned out to be the case. My husband wasn't totally surprised, but the rest of the family seemed shocked. Thankfully, they've gotten over it, and Evan fits right in."

"So it's a happy ending." Echo smiles like she's glad for them, but isn't sure why Keeley told the story.

That makes two of us.

"Yes, but it's not the end. A few months later, Evan was approached by a woman in a parking lot. Bethany—that's her name—told Evan they share the same father. We were all stunned to learn she was right. Honestly, it's been an adjustment for each of them to find out they have unexpected siblings. But Bethany fits with the rest of the clan. In fact, they all get along amazingly well, despite having such different upbringings. My point is…the unexpected isn't always a bad thing."

From inside the house, a wide-shouldered guy with light brown hair, a sharp jaw, and a thousand-dollar suit approaches us. He looks solemn and resolute. "We'll take it from here, sunshine." Then he turns to Xavian, hand outstretched. "Hi, I'm Maxon Reed. Apparently, I'm your oldest brother."

* * * *

Oh, shit. I didn't see that coming. I should have, given Keeley's story and Xavian's situation…

X stands, gaping as he shakes Maxon's hand automatically. "You're…my brother?"

"One of them, yes. I hired Mr. Sakamoto, the private detective who reached out to you."

"*We* hired him." A slightly younger carbon copy of Maxon with darker hair saunters closer, backing him up. "I'm Griffin Reed, also your brother."

Xavian looks shaken as he takes the guy's hand next.

A drop-dead gorgeous brunette sidles between them. "And I'm Harlow Reed—well, Weston now—one of your two sisters."

Even if they didn't have the blood tests to back them up, I'd know they were telling the truth because they all have piercing eyes in the same unusual shade of green.

Just like Xavian.

"I-I have *three* siblings?" X stammers out, clearly floored.

He's still cautious, and I get it. Who knows what these people want? Why are they introducing themselves now?

"Um…remember my story?" Keeley gives Xavian an encouraging

smile.

It takes X a few seconds to process that. "Shit. There are more."

As he's reeling, another guy jogs in and shoulders his way past the others to Xavian's side. He's younger than Maxon and Griff. Taller, too. And somehow sharp and gawky at once. Echo would probably call him nerd-hot. And yep, he has the same green eyes. "Evan Cook. I wasn't raised with these three"—he crooks a thumb at the Reed siblings—"so if they're assholes, that's just them."

The others laugh, and I'm confused about why that's a joke until Maxon clears it up. "We all have Dad's blood running through our veins. So we have to fight the asshole DNA, you included, genius." He turns to Xavian, brow raised. "You get accused of being a selfish dick often?"

I bark out a laugh. I know X well, so I see through his BS, but… "All the time. I'm his friend, Hayes Elliot. And this is Echo Hope."

Echo stands to shake Maxon's hand. "I'm Eryn Quaid's sister."

Maxon's grin widens. "What a damn small world. It's nice to meet you." Then he turns his focus on Xavian again. "Between the eyes and the attitude, I'd know you're a Reed even without the blood test."

A blonde, a few years older than Harlow, who looks as intelligent as she is beautiful, joins the others. Her eyes are gray swathed with the family green, and a smile plays at her lips. "Bethany Holmes. Just so you know, these guys are all assholes. Harlow and I are angels."

The others scoff, laughing in good-natured fun. It's clear they're a close-knit bunch.

Xavian looks overwhelmed. "So…I have five siblings? Holy shit. That's a lot."

Griff clears his throat, then casts a glance to the parking lot. Relief relaxes his features. "Six—that we know of. Here comes the other one."

A petite blonde carrying a little boy heads our way, backed up by a tall, lanky guy in a Hawaiian shirt with a loose-hipped swagger. As they get closer, I rule him out as a brother since Maxon said he was the oldest, and this guy has him beat by roughly five years. A glance at the woman tells me she's probably not related to the others, either. Unlike Bethany and Harlow, she's a waif. And she has striking eyes in an icy blue.

But the little boy she's holding? Green eyes.

"The kid is my brother, too?" Xavian's jaw falls open.

"Yes, I'm Amanda. And this little guy is my son, Oliver," the dainty blonde offers. "Your mother, like Evan's, Bethany's, and I were all, at one time or another, employed as Barclay's personal assistant. I just happened to be one of the last."

"Wait." Xavian steps back, stunned and blinking. "You mean you're all related to Barclay Reed? The guy who swindled his clients out of hundreds of millions of dollars? The Bernie Madoff of the West Coast. *That* Barclay Reed?"

"Ah, so you've heard of our 'esteemed' father," Harlow says tartly. "That's him. He was a real peach. Maxon, Griff, and I grew up with him, so we speak from experience. But he fucked us all over in one way or another." Her gaze slides over to her sister. "Probably Bethany most."

Xavian scans the group, taking in one face after the other, in stupefied shock. "Wow. Okay, so…what do you all want from me? I don't know anything about Barclay Reed. I never met him. He was just some guy I heard about on the news. So I don't have a story to tell the press about him for a buck. My mom probably could have, but she passed away three years ago. If you're worried I'll talk or something, don't be. I've got nothing to say."

Keeley, who's been quiet for most of the introductions, speaks again. "Nobody wants anything from you."

He stares at the group suspiciously, then glances around the big, multimillion dollar house. "If you're worried I'm going to somehow try to cash in on the notoriety of being one of Barclay Reed's offspring, that's not happening, either. I work in the investment sector, so attaching myself to that name wouldn't exactly help me gain my clients' trust."

The redhead glances at her husband, then back to Xavian with a sigh. "We just want to get to know you. You're family."

Keeley said the magic words.

Xavian visibly thaws. "Seriously? That's it?"

Evan answers first. "I lost my mom at five, and other than one foster mom I was close to, I had no family. When I met the Reed clan, I'd just lost my first wife and unborn child in a car accident. I had no one, and Maxon, Griff, and Harlow all welcomed me…so I moved here from Seattle with my current wife a few months back."

Bethany nods. "I left LA after my life as Barclay's right hand ended with his arrest and all the awful accusations in the press. I'd met Evan once. I'd never set eyes on any of the others." She nods toward the Reed siblings. "It was Christmas, I was broke, and I had nowhere to go. They took me in. And suddenly, I was part of the family. My husband and I moved here soon after."

Xavian gets really quiet. I'm sure it's hard for him to believe they don't want anything, but I actually think they're sincere.

"I'm not related to any of them," Amanda puts in. "Harlow and I grew up together."

"We've been friends since we were kids." The pretty brunette grabs Amanda's hand. "We still are."

She squeezes it back. "And I regret betraying that friendship to have a relationship with her father, but I can't regret Oliver. These people have all welcomed my fiancé and me as family. They didn't judge. They simply listened when we needed it. They helped when we were lost. They're what family should be."

Xavian scrubs a hand over his face. He's overwhelmed. It's a lot to take in, and he won't know them well enough to trust them unless he spends more time with them.

I stand and address the Reed clan. "Can you excuse us for a moment?"

After their murmured assent, Xavian follows me down to the shore. I glance back to check on Echo, but she's already fallen into an animated conversation with Keeley. Harlow quickly joins in with Bethany listening intently.

I turn to X, who's totally shellshocked. "You okay?"

"I don't know what to think. Whether to believe them…"

"Only you can answer that, but I think you should. At the least, a conversation won't hurt. You have a great nose for bullshit. Use it."

He pulls his phone from his pocket. "No time. We gotta get back for this shindig."

"I think it's more important for you to get to know these people while we're on the island. You can talk to the CEO another day."

Xavian sighs. "You're right."

Together, we head back to the group. As soon as I reach Echo, I hold out my hand and help her to her feet. "It was great meeting you all. We've got a mixer to attend. A work thing. We can come back for Xavian in a few hours."

He'll need more time than that to make up his mind, but it's a start.

"How about tomorrow?" Keeley suggests hopefully.

"We don't have any vacancies, sunshine," Maxon reminds.

"And no one wants to come to my house." Griff grimaces. "I have two boys under the age of four and a pregnant woman puking up her toenails. Speaking of which, I need to call and check on Britta. Excuse me." He pulls his phone free and steps into the house.

"He can stay with Nia and me," Evan offers. "We have spare rooms."

"Clint and I have room, too," Bethany offers, then strokes her still-flat stomach. "But this baby is sapping all my energy. I keep falling into bed, exhausted, when everyone's toddlers do."

The group laughs, and the women assure her it will get better.

"He should stay with Noah and me," Harlow says, then turns to Xavian. "Nolan, our son, is finally sleeping through the night, so it will be restful. And we have the best private oceanfront views on the island…"

Really? How is that possible without a shit-ton of money?

X seems to have the same question and reaches a conclusion before me. "Hold up. Noah…Weston? You're married to *the* Noah Weston? The quarterback? The future hall-of-famer?"

"Yep, that's him. I was never into football, so when we met he was just an oversized jock with an oversized house and an oversized ego. But he's grown on me a little." She winks.

Clearly that's true—since she has a giant rock on her finger, and they have a baby together.

Xavian's eyes look ready to pop free. "He won't mind?"

"If he does, I have ways of persuading him." Harlow flashes a salacious grin.

Her adult brothers collectively groan. Even Oliver starts fussing.

"Ugh, I don't want to hear that shit," Maxon grouses.

Griff and Evan both shake their heads, wearing matching grimaces.

Harlow and Bethany laugh. Keeley high-fives her sisters-in-law. Xavian looks fascinated by their interaction.

"What do you say?" Harlow asks him.

"I appreciate the offer. All right."

Smiling, I clap X on the shoulder. He's making the right choice. Hopefully, time with his surprisingly big brood of family will be good for him.

Unfortunately, after this mixer is over, I'll have hours and hours alone with Echo. Plenty of time to fuck up…

"Why don't you call when you're ready to come back to the hotel? We'll pick you up."

"Or one of us can bring him to you." Maxon shrugs. "Whatever you want, Xavian. We're just hoping for some time to get to know you."

"Sure." X nods like he's still processing the fact that, in the snap of a finger, he went from being an only child and an orphan to being surrounded by family. "I'm down for that."

Immediately, the rest of the big group invites themselves to Harlow and Noah's place for dinner.

"You ready to head back?" I murmur to Echo.

She nods, so happy for Xavian that she's wearing her huge heart all over her face. "Yeah."

We wave to the others, then head for the convertible. Automatically, my arm slips around her waist. My hand affixes to the curve of her hip. And I try to tamp down my dangerous excitement for the night to come, but by the time we're in the car I'm already sweating and hard.

I need a plan—quick. Going to the mixer will eat up an hour or two of our evening…but then what? Echo and I will be completely alone all night. If I don't control what we do together and how badly I want her, I could fuck up everything. On the other hand, if I avoid touching her for my sanity, she'll know I was lying. She'll feel played. She'll be mad and hurt. Her confidence will take a blow.

I sigh. I have to tread carefully or I'll lose my best friend forever.

Chapter Six

"This afternoon was crazy," Echo remarks from behind the bathroom door.

I glance at my watch. Ten after five. We're late. Typical Echo. She drives my inner taskmaster insane, but her tardiness is a quirk I'm used to. Sometimes, it's almost cute…just not when I'm hoping to get some face-time with the big boss. Since he's based in New York, not the West Coast, my chances to schmooze him are limited.

But Echo has this way about her… It's almost impossible to stay angry. I always end up forgiving her. The universe does, too, because it frequently rewards her gentle bending of the rules with something fabulously serendipitous.

Taking a deep breath, I force myself to relax. We'll get to the mixer. It's not like I'm eager for the actual event. These things are boring, full of windbags, and seem to last forever.

"Insane," I answer through the door. "What are the odds of Xavian being related to that inn keeper's husband and having so much family?"

"Right? But I have a good feeling about it. X needs relatives he can count on, and Eryn swears the Reeds are solid."

"Plus, with Noah Weston for a brother-in-law, he'll always be popular with the jocks in the office."

"Um…is that Noah guy a big deal?"

I laugh. Echo has never been into watching sports. She'd rather participate. "Huge. Probably one of the top five pro quarterbacks of all time."

"Oh. Well, I'm just happy that the family seems willing to make room for him."

"One hundred percent." I glance at my watch again. Now we're fifteen minutes late. It will still take at least another five to walk to the ballroom. I'm getting antsy.

As if she can read my mind, Echo laughs. "You're about to pace, aren't you? I'm almost ready."

From the other side of the door, I hear clothing rustle. That's all it takes for my subversive imagination to melt thoughts of business from my brain and start feeding me visions of Echo. I picture her sliding on a lacy bra that cups her full breasts—which I'm ashamed to say I want to touch—and matching underwear that shields her innocent pussy. Mentally, I examine every curve, just like I did when she wore that barely legal bikini. But now it's better...and worse. In this vision, I can see through everything.

Lust jolts me. I curl my hands into fists to restrain myself from marching into the bathroom, pressing her against the nearest flat surface, and stripping off whatever she just put on.

If simply imagining her in next to nothing is making you crazy, what will the real thing do?

Deep breaths. I need to slow my roll. I can't be this hot for Echo. I'm not having sex with my best friend.

When she pushes the bathroom door open, my mental pep talk goes out the window. Her dress is a transparent lacy shift in creamy white with a sheath underneath that's the same color as her skin. The effect, along with the plunging neckline and short skirt, leaves her looking hazardously close to naked. The erection I was trying to will away turns steely.

She's wound her hair into a soft twist and left loose tendrils framing her face. Her eyes are shaded in a smudged brown with a hit of nude shimmer on her lids. I fall into her stare and get lost. Somehow, I manage to pull free, and I trip visually on her rosy lips. They make me ache to kiss her again.

For the first time I can ever remember, she's wearing high heels. They're strappy things that match her dress, wrap around her ankles, and make her legs look sinfully long.

"Wow." The word slips out as I gawk.

She smiles, flashing me her dimple again. "Thanks. Shall we?"

"Sure." Staying here would be dangerous to my sanity...and her virginity.

From the table, she grabs a little crocheted purse. I open the door before following her out—and get another surprise.

"The back of your dress is missing."

Echo laughs and wraps her hand around my arm, pulling me down the hall.

I'm serious. Everything between the shoulder blades and the curve of her ass is bare. Another reality hits me. "You can't possibly be wearing a bra."

She sends me a flirty smile. "No, I can't."

I stop in my tracks. "This mixer is optional, shortcake. We could stay in and…" I sidle closer and graze my lips up her neck before I can stop myself.

"No. You only have two events to attend all week, and I'm going to show off this dress I fell in love with to someone."

"Oh, I'm looking at it." Even though I shouldn't.

Echo grins and tugs on my arm. "Come on…"

With a rough sigh, I follow her to the elevator, then down to the ballroom, already brimming with my co-workers and some of their plus-ones. The younger, single guys, mostly my friends from different offices, congregate around the bar, shooting back whiskey, talking bullshit, and clandestinely browsing the handful of single ladies who work in this largely male environment all dressed up for the cocktail party.

My CEO, along with the senior management team, stands at the door, shaking hands.

When I reach his side, he claps my shoulder with a wide smile. "Elliot! Good to see you."

"Thanks, Mr. Helm. This is Echo Hope. She just graduated from my alma mater last week."

"Congratulations!"

"Thanks." She sends him a dimpled smile as she shakes his hand. "Nice to meet you."

"Glad you could join us. You enjoying Maui?"

"It's amazing." She sighs. "We got out to sightsee and visit some people I know on the island today. But before I leave, I'm determined to teach Hayes how to surf."

"You surf?" Mr. Helm looks impressed.

"I learned as a kid. It's awesome fun. A good way to be with nature, you know? And great for building core strength."

My boss nods like she's right, then he looks my way. "Now I'm jealous. Sounds like you're going to have a great teacher."

"If you want to learn, I'm happy to teach you, too."

More bonding time with the CEO would be great, but he's recently divorced and reportedly on the prowl. He's not looking at Echo like he's interested…yet. But if he saw her in a bikini?

"I'm sure he's busy, shortcake."

Mr. Helm smiles wryly. "I am, but I hope you'll tell me all about it at the closing mixer. If Elliot is half as determined on a surfboard as he is in the office, I'm sure he'll do great."

"Thank you, sir." I hustle Echo along before my boss changes his mind.

"Great meeting you!" she calls over her shoulder.

I guide her into the ballroom where the deejay is blasting some eighties tune about Walking on Sunshine and head toward the bar. Instantly, my work buddies stare at Echo. I know those hungry expressions. They're sharks. That's why they're great at making money. They also skim the singles' pool looking for the tastiest morsels before consuming them whole and shitting them out.

They aren't getting anywhere near her.

After the two of us grab drinks, I give my work pals a vague wave and lead her to a group I don't normally socialize with: the thirty-somethings. They're largely married with kids. They spend fewer hours in the office and are less relentless for the financial kill, but they're also less likely to hit on Echo. We'll stay at this gathering long enough not to be rude. Then I'll take her to dinner. Maybe I can suggest a movie, too. Or could I get her drunk enough to pass out? Then I wouldn't have to worry about her tempting me beyond my control.

"Hey, Elliot!" calls Dave Crenshaw. He's a decent guy from the San Diego office who trained me my first few days on the job.

"Hey, man." We shake hands and bump shoulders. "What's up?"

"Just enjoying the time with my wife before the baby comes in September. Work kicked my ass when we got married so we didn't get much of a honeymoon." He introduces me to his other half, Aubrey.

"This is"—What do I call her since she temporarily agreed to be more than my friend?—"Echo."

She smiles warmly. "We've been friends forever. Congratulations on your baby. Have you decided on a name?"

Just like that, the conversation is off and running. Another couple joins us. Then another from the office in the Valley. I came to the mixer thinking I'd shake Mr. Helm's hand and hang with my buddies for a bit.

But I can hear them now, loud and shitfaced, verbally undressing the waitstaff in skirts. God, am I ever that obnoxious?

I've always thought mixing it up with the old-and-marrieds would be dull as fuck, but I've already made two contacts, got an offer to work on a joint deal, and an invitation to play poker in a couple of weeks. And they aren't slackers in the office at all. The guy I just met from Orange County tripled the commission I made last year. I'm in awe.

Echo already seems to be fast friends with their wives. I've heard talk about visiting a yoga studio back home. My girl knows someone who can paint a mural for another mom who wants one in her toddler's room. She's also connecting Kella, who's got a side-hustle as a web developer, with another wife who's starting a home-based vegan skincare business. Then the group invites us to dinner after the mixer, and Echo is on board. Spending more time with these folks is a guilty relief.

As we leave, I ignore the ribbing from my usual pals still hanging by the bar, drinking the company booze, and get an approving thumbs-up from Mr. Helm.

Dinner with everyone is great. By the time it's over, Echo also has connections for gently used play equipment for her new employers. Best of all, she smiled the whole evening.

On the way to our bank of elevators, I reaffirm my game plan: put her in an orgasm coma while keeping my pants zipped, then take a self-pleasuring shower afterward and shake off any sexual thoughts I have. Tomorrow…I'll figure out how to recycle the strategy so my best friend leaves Hawaii as virginal as the day she arrived. I've recovered from my earlier lascivious thoughts. I'm braced now.

Confident, I take her hand. But I'm startled again by the sudden awareness that zips and hums between us.

"Thanks for coming with me," I say.

"Of course. It was fun, except…" A blush stains her cheeks. "The women asked me how long we'd been together. I did my best to be non-committal."

I got speculative glances, too. Guys don't usually ask, but I could tell they had questions. "I'm sure you did great."

The elevator doors open, and we step in. We're totally alone since it's late. Time to put my plan in motion.

I back Echo against the wall of the ascending car, take her face in my hands, and press my body to hers. I'm more eager to touch her than I should be. The instant I do, my control starts to slip.

It's not a good sign.

"Your mouth is driving me crazy, shortcake. Do us both a favor, and tell me not to kiss you."

Her lips part gently. Her tongue peeks out to wet them.

My body tightens.

"Why would I do that when I'm aching for you to kiss me?"

Shit.

I still my hand around her nape and lift her face to mine. Her plump lips part gently. Her lashes flutter. Her breathing quickens.

It's only a kiss. We're in semi-public. It can't get too crazy, right?

But nothing with Echo is ever "normal."

Before I can take her mouth, she lifts on her tiptoes and fuses her lips to mine. They're soft, pillowy, and warm. Right on cue, that sweet, sweet scent of hers fills my nose. Then she wraps her arms around my neck with a little moan and plasters her breasts against me. The points of her nipples drill into my chest.

Is it hot in this elevator, or is it just me?

Somehow, she nestles even closer. Every curve of her body fits against a plane of mine. Then she wriggles like she's dying to get closer. Tingles rush through me. My blood heats. My cock nearly bursts through my zipper. Hunger surges. I stop thinking as I grip her hips and press her to my aching shaft. Echo doesn't protest, just gasps into my kiss and melts against me.

The little ding announcing that the elevator has reached our floor makes me snarl with frustration. The doors start to slide shut again when I lift Echo and carry her out. We step onto the breezeway as the car disappears, panting hard and staring at each other.

Her eyes search mine, earnest and dark with desire.

Would it be so terrible if I gave Echo what she wants? What her eyes are pleading for right now?

Yes. Forget your cock. Think of your best friend.

"Come on." My voice sounds both soft and scratchy as I take her hand and lead her to our room.

When we step inside, the radio she left on in the background belts out Harry Styles's summery, sexual "Watermelon Sugar." The song matches our mood.

"Hayes?" she murmurs as I lock the door behind us.

The desire dripping from her voice makes me stiffen. "Yeah, shortcake?"

"It's going to hurt the first time, right?"

The thought of Echo losing her virginity kills me because she'll be with someone else. But that's best for her, so I tamp down my violent thoughts and this weird jealousy.

"Yeah, but we don't have to rush into this."

She drops her purse on the nearby table and pads back to me. "We're not rushing. I'm ready."

I was afraid she was going to say that.

Time to start the next phase of my plan: pour her some wine, kiss her thoroughly, put my hand under her skirt, give her an orgasm or two—and hope she falls asleep. Rinse and repeat for the rest of the week.

But as usual, Echo destroys my carefully laid plans.

Reaching behind her neck, she unfastens her dress. I hold my breath as she pulls one arm free, then the other. The bodice falls to her waist, completely exposing her pale breasts and their juicy, berry-tipped nipples.

Oh, holy shit.

I'm in trouble.

"Shortcake…" I scrub a hand across my face and stare. I can't move. Or breathe. Hell, I don't even want to blink and miss a second of her.

Biting her lip in the shadowy room, Echo reaches around to the small of her back. A quiet hiss tells me she's drawing down the zipper.

"Wait. Let me do that." Later. Much later.

But it's already too late.

The lacy dress slides down her thighs and pools at her feet. Then she's wearing nothing but high heels and a pair of panties the same color as her flesh. The front panel is simple. Plain cotton with a tiny silk bow directly beneath her belly button. Unlike my fantasies, the fabric isn't transparent, but reality proves excruciatingly sexier because I can't see her pussy. What I *can* see? The tight fabric clinging to her swollen folds and an obvious wet spot.

She's that aroused, and I've barely touched her?

Knowing I'm the man turning her on stomps all over my good intentions.

She steps out of her dress, trembling as she turns to drape the garment over a chair. I get a look at the lush jut of her ass. The simple cotton fronting her panties is gone, replaced by a sheet of lace so delicate and thin I see every inch of the high, firm flesh flaring between her hips, the delicate line bisecting those juicy globes beneath her tiny waist, and the round cheeks curving below the edge of the lace, leading my stare directly to the shadows between her thighs that shield her untouched pussy. Suddenly, I want to see it, touch it, taste it, and take it—way more than I should.

Dragging in a breath, I try to form words—hell, thoughts—when she steps out of her shoes and closes the six feet between us on soft, silent feet. She stops short of touching me. "Say something."

"You're so fucking beautiful, I can't speak."

She smiles. It's not her everyday grin. And it's nothing like the face she makes when she's about to laugh. It's not the strained curl of her lips I've seen when she tries to skate through an uncomfortable situation. It's definitely not an expression she's plastered on to placate me. This smile is big and real. It makes her glow. "You think so?"

"Yeah." My insistence makes her smile even brighter. That does something to me. "You're the most beautiful woman I've ever seen."

I probably shouldn't have admitted that, but I won't lie to her…at least not more than I have to.

She frowns. "Now I know you're being less than honest."

I catch her chin in my grip and lift it until she's forced to look at me. "I'm not. Until this week, I had no idea how stunning you are, Echo."

She searches my eyes breathlessly as she reaches for the buttons of my dress shirt. "Are you going to take your clothes off?"

If she gets me naked, my plan will go sideways. I feel like a class-A bastard, but I don't merely want her. I'm dying to worship her body. And the urge isn't just about her looks. She's staring at me with uncertain eyes, and everything inside me aches to hold her, to prove to her that I find her desirable. Beautiful. Lovable. I might not cherish her in the til-death-do-us-part sense, but I care enough about her to make damn sure her first time is the best it can be. Maybe that's enough?

Nope. I'm rationalizing again. I need to stop.

Gently but firmly, I grab her wrists. "Eventually."

"Are you going to touch me?"

"Yes." I doubt anything, even guilt, can stop me now.

Finally, I lift my hands to her body, shocked to find I'm shaking. Instantly, my palms cup her breasts, and she fills them. Echo is more than a handful.

Her eyes slide shut. She sighs out a shaky moan. The sound slides all the way through my body.

You're fondling your best friend.

And I'm so fucking aroused by her, I barely manage to stop from stripping off every stitch I'm wearing and carrying her to bed.

Shit, I have to get myself under control. It shouldn't be this difficult. I'm not hard up. Three short days ago, I stopped by Jayci's place to get a little before I headed out for a sexless week in Hawaii. I left satisfied enough. It should have tided me over for a mere seven days.

But I never suspected I'd be unexpectedly fixated by my gorgeous best friend.

"Hayes…"

Her plea sounds breathy and desperate. I can't resist that.

I slide my thumbs over her nipples, gratified when they stiffen even more under my touch. I'm torn between kissing her, sucking on them, or just staring.

Echo takes the decision from me, pressing closer and tilting her lips under mine.

Lowering my head, I close the distance between our mouths and send my lips crashing over hers without finesse or restraint. She whimpers and opens to me, luring me deeper, inviting me to take more.

Yes. Fuck yes.

Our kiss spirals out of control in seconds. Desire scalds me. I'm on fire. It's surreal. This is Echo, my best friend since childhood.

Right now, I fucking want her so badly I'm shaking and sweating. But I shouldn't make her mine in every way if I'm not going to make her mine forever. So I have to settle for making her feel good this week…and hope that's enough.

Without ending the kiss, I lift her, carrying her to the sofa and plopping down on the cushions. She tumbles onto me, straddling my hips and falling deeper into my kiss as she presses herself against my cock. Without missing a beat, she wriggles against me. Her little catches of breath, along with her hard nipples burning my palms, crush my best intentions.

Realizing how gorgeous Echo is shocks me, but seeing that she's also sexy as fuck? Mind. Blown. She oozes female. And sex. Echo might be a virgin, but she's clearly not self-conscious about her body, afraid of what might happen next, or remotely shy. She moves in the perfect rhythm to simulate sex—and drives me out of my head.

I need to get control of this situation or…

Best not to think about the "or" right now.

Reluctantly, I grab her hips to still them and ease back from her lips. "Slow down, shortcake."

"Why?"

Because I'm trying not to fuck you isn't the answer she wants to hear. "Let me make you feel good first."

"You are," she swears as she tears into the buttons of my dress shirt with feverish fingers. "You will."

She's released a few by the time I grab her hands and stop her. But as soon as I let go of her hips, she gyrates on my cock again. Fresh desire rips through me. I toss back my head and groan.

Fuck it. She can have the shirt.

With her hips in my hands again, I slow her rocking. If I had better control of myself, I'd let her work against me until she came. I'm shocked I don't, but there it is. Besides, I'd rather give her pleasure with my hands. Or my mouth.

Why not both?

My head down south thinks that's a great plan. My befuddled brain jumps on board.

Without another thought, I flip her down to the sofa and half-press myself on top of her. My lips unerringly capture hers again. And my hand wanders from her hard-tipped tits, over the flat surface of her stomach, and straight under the waistband of her panties.

Then…oh, fuck. I'm. Touching. Echo's. Pussy.

And she's drenched. She's smooth and bare, too.

When I graze her steely clit, she gasps. Desire jerks against my mental restraint.

"Shortcake…"

"Oh, my god. Hayes…yes. Yes!"

She spreads herself open wider, inviting me to do whatever I want. She trusts me, and I feel horrible for lying—but that won't stop me from making her come. I'll apologize later.

"So fucking perfect," I praise her as I settle my fingers between her folds, mesmerized by the jolt of her hips in rhythm with my slow, tormenting circles. "Jesus, Echo."

Her back arches. Her body shudders. She clutches my shoulders, her eyes flaring wide as she whimpers for me. "You're going to make me come."

Already? Damn it. Some wretched part of me wants this to last all night so I can hear her beg, plead, and whimper until she can't help but scream.

I don't dare.

"Good. Let go," I murmur against her lips before I seize them again, plowing deep, tongues tangling, while my fingers work her closer to frenzy.

She pants and gasps, rolling her hips again and seeking out my touch. Fuck, I want her panties off. I want to watch my fingers in her pussy. I want to see her totally naked, flushed, and aching for me.

I want inside her.

This isn't about you.

I step up my effort, kissing down to her chin, gliding over the graceful arch of her exposed throat, to the swells of her breasts…then finally to her nipples desperately stabbing the air.

The moment I take one in my mouth, her clit swells under my fingers, which I work faster and harder. She keens out. I nearly lose it.

She's so responsive. Fuck, she's on the edge. Her sugary scent hangs thick. Then I realize what I've been smelling on her all week is her pussy. It's perfuming the air, filling my nose, getting me high. It's threatening to override what little control I have left.

I lave her nipple, then move to the other. They're so fucking hard against my tongue. I'm probably going to hell for this, but I suck the nub deep. She keens. Her hips lift and strain. Her pussy is soaked. And she grabs me like only I can save her.

She's seconds from orgasm.

Electricity fills the air. Her need threatens to mow me down. I've never felt so dialed into a woman. I'm two seconds away from tearing off her panties and telling my good intentions to fuck off.

But she squeezes her eyes shut. Her clit turns impossibly hard. Her entire body goes taut, legs stiffening as she pings with climax. And she screams. My name. At the top of her lungs.

I've never been more turned on in my life.

It's a dangerous realization as I drag out her pleasure through a long, grinding, throaty climax that seems to roll on for half an eternity before she falls completely limp in my arms.

Endless, panting moments later, she opens her heavy-lidded eyes with a loopy smile. A satisfied Echo takes my breath away. Right now, I'd kill to put that expression on her face every day.

"That was"—she sighs—"Amazing. I need to return the favor."

I'd love that, but no. Hell no. If I get any hotter, I seriously doubt I'll be able to resist.

I've got to stop her.

As always, Echo has a mind of her own. She slides off the couch between my legs—and onto her knees. Then she reaches for my zipper.

My heart stops. My breath saws in and out of my chest as I grab her wrists. "Echo. Shortcake…"

Her golden eyes climb to my face, wide and supplicating. "Let me make you feel good. Let me try…"

How the fuck do I say no to that?

"I don't know how good my self-control is right now."

She gives me a soft smile of understanding. "That's okay. I don't want your self-control. I just want you."

My grip tightens. I'm desperate. Maybe I should put my tongue on her pussy and drive her to distraction. I'd love to try…but if I don't let her touch me now, will I spend the rest of my life wondering what her hands on my cock feel like?

It's a dangerous question. I'm an asshole for even thinking it. "Are you sure?"

Echo nods earnestly.

I'm insane, but slowly, I release her.

She rips my button free, yanks down my zipper, and frees my erection. Instantly, she grips it, wrapping her small hands around me and stroking with a slow, barely there touch that wrenches a groan from me. I sink down the cushions and lift my hips, silently urging her on.

"You're so hard. But your skin is so soft here." Wonder fills her voice.

"Yep," I barely manage to eke out.

"And you're wet." She skates a slow, sliding thumb over my sensitive head. "Leaking."

I hiss and struggle to think of a way to take back control of the situation. "Don't do that."

She stops instantly. "You don't like it?"

It would be smarter to lie to her, but… "No, it feels too good. I'm most sensitive there."

"Really?" she drawls like she finds that information very helpful—then drags her thumb over my crest in a horribly delicious, spine-bending glide.

"Fuck." It's torture.

I throw my head back, dizzy and reeling. But every moment she's touching me is a moment she isn't expecting me to take her virginity. I've just got to hold out…somehow.

Then again, if she makes me come, I can tell her I'm spent and couldn't possibly get hard again tonight—a total lie—but at this point that might be my best option.

"That feels incredible, shortcake," I groan. "You have no idea…"

She giggles. "Since you just gave me an orgasm, I do. It's your turn."

Before I can grasp what Echo has planned, she raises on her knees, lowers her head, and, oh—holy motherfucking son of a bitch—closes her lips around me.

I've died. I'm in heaven. And I never want to leave.

Then her warm, wet mouth descends so slowly down my cock, I'd swear she's determined to taste every inch along the way. I drag in a breath, trying to steady myself. But it's no use. My fingers thrust into her hair, sending bobby pins flying and her skeins tumbling down. I shove my fingers in the thick mass and fist it as her lips nearly reach the bottom of my shaft.

Yes. Fuck yes.

That's your best friend giving you a blow job.

Yeah, and I can't remember a woman's mouth ever making me ache like this.

As if I have no control, my hips rise to meet her. She takes the rest of my cock deep, her tongue cradling me before she sucks me like she can't get enough. She whimpers. Her eyes lift to me. She's seeking my approval.

Suddenly, I have no filter, and I can't find a single fuck to give about what happens tomorrow.

"Echo… Suck me. Yes. All the way to the tip. Hard. Like that. Oh, fuck…"

She does it exactly the way I ask, but when her lips reach the head again, she swirls her tongue across the sensitive surface. A gentle glide of her teeth follows.

I nearly come out of my skin.

Her mouth heads straight back down, this time faster, skimming my length, dragging in audible breaths through her nose as she angles me all the way to the back of her throat.

Where the fuck did she learn that?

Before I can ask, she starts in on me again.

Another few pulls, and I'll be a goner.

Just when I swore this couldn't get any hotter, she slips one hand inside her panties and touches herself. Her head bobbing on my cock and her hand moving between her legs mesmerize me. I give in to the moment, letting my head fall back and my eyes slide shut. Fire licks its way up my shaft, blazing through my bloodstream. I spread my legs. My fingers tighten in her hair. A groan tears from my throat.

She's killing me, especially when her frantic, breathy gasps tell me her excitement is ramping up as quickly as mine.

Then the rhythm of her mouth falters. She laves my head with a hard, shallow suck and pauses. Finally, after a moan, she sinks down. Then she stops, shaking.

I open my eyes. The sight of Echo is a gut-punch of arousal, but the needs of her trembling body are overriding the coordination of her mouth. I'm not surprised. She's not used to pleasuring anyone but herself.

Whatever. I'm more than willing to help her along.

Gently, I tug on her hair and brace a finger under her chin, lifting her off me slowly. She looks at me with dazed, dilated eyes, her hand still moving between her legs. She whimpers, her face full of agony.

I can't leave her like this. Hell, I shouldn't even be taking pleasure from her in the first place…but I can't stop myself.

"Come here, shortcake." I sit up and pull her closer.

She looks crestfallen. "I wasn't doing it right?"

"You were doing great." I grin. "Until you got distracted."

"I'm sorry. I'll stop touching…" She halts mid-sentence, flushing a deeper red. "I'll do better."

"Let me improve your focus." I don't question how risky my next move is. I just slide the soaking panties off her hips and down her thighs.

"What are you going to do?"

Her voice is breathy and husky. It torques me with fresh desire.

I don't bother to answer, just grin as I wrap my arms around her and lift her onto the sofa, facing me on her knees. She frowns, confused, until I inch down, sliding my ass to the edge of the cushion and stare at her pussy right above my parted lips.

She's so swollen and pink, juicy, soft, and completely smooth. Does she have any idea how much I want her?

Echo gasps when she realizes my intent, her indrawn breath sharp and shocked. "You don't have to—"

"I want to. Don't make me stop."

I grip her thighs and lift my head, then drag my tongue through her slick slit.

Perfect. That's the only way I can describe Echo's taste.

I dive deeper, get more of her on my tongue. She's hot. Sweet as honey. Addicting. I need more—now.

She grabs on to the back of the sofa with a long, agonized groan that urges me on.

I prod her pebbled clit, and she shudders. I want more. I open her pussy wide with my thumbs, settle the flat of my tongue inside her furrow, and cover every wet inch of her in a long, slow lick.

Her thighs tremble. She chants my name like she's hoping I'll save her. But I want her to burn.

I eat at her hungrily, tasting, sucking, sampling, exploring until she gasps in increasingly high-pitched breaths. Her legs shudder. Her breasts bob. Her clit turns to stone.

Then Echo tosses her head back and screams.

She looks so fucking beautiful in pleasure… Even if I live to be a hundred and even if I fuck a thousand women, I will never forget Echo in this moment.

As she comes down from her loud, shattering climax, I tuck away the implications of that realization, sit up, and try to take her in my arms.

But Echo has already escaped, slid back to her knees at my feet, and started sucking on my cock with a desperation that literally steals my breath.

Any cool-down the pause in her oral adulation gave me is gone. Less than a half-dozen pulls with her mouth, and I'm lifting to her rhythm, breathing like a bellows, and swearing that my best friend is about to steal my sanity with this mind-melting pleasure.

Maybe that's not all she's stealing…

"Echo. Suck me. That's it. Fuck. Fuck! Oh, my god… Yes! Ahh…"

The pressure coiling and building inside me suddenly explodes. Violent need swirls, churning in my balls and knocking me on my ass. Liquid ecstasy jets, drowning my good sense.

Echo is with me, not skipping a beat, despite how rough my grip in her hair is or how insistently I push into her warm, waiting mouth.

When it's over, I pant, watching, stunned, as she sits up, swallows, and smiles at me like I've somehow made her life complete.

Suddenly, I have the sneaking suspicion that mine never will be if we try going back to simply being friends.

Chapter Seven

Sun seeps through the blackout drapes as I toss and turn restlessly. Something nags at my half-awake consciousness. I'll have to face whatever it is when I get up, but I doze and ignore it a bit longer.

Until a very naked woman curls herself against me, warm and soft, her head nestling on my arm and her tits plastered to my chest. I open my eyes.

Echo.

Last night rushes back to me. Her undressing. Her screaming in pleasure. Her mouth on me.

Oh. My. God.

I stop breathing and stare. She looks like the best friend I've had since we bonded over being the new kids at a new school. The wavy hair she's bitched about a hundred times curls away from the sleep-soft face I've seen nearly every day for a decade and a half. I shouldn't be freaking out.

But I am, because no matter how familiar Echo is, I'll never look at her the same.

This morning, I notice things about her I never have. Though she's all woman, her long, dark lashes brush round cheeks that are almost girlish. Her lips are rosy, the bottom one heavy and pouty when it parts slightly, as if in unspoken invitation. Her bare shoulder is dotted with two tiny freckles, which peek out above the crisp white sheet covering the rest of her body. Not that it does any good. Last night, I saw her. I felt her. And I remember her—every detail. I don't know how I'll forget.

We can't ever go back to being just friends. I'm not sure I want to.

In my arms, Echo smells like sweet female. My erection, which isn't simply morning wood, prods her, desperate to know what being joined with her feels like. She'd let me take her. In fact, she'd welcome me if I rolled her onto her back, spread her legs, and pushed deep inside her. The thought makes me even harder.

But I can't do that unless I'm willing to gamble our lifelong friendship that I'm the right man for her.

The prospect is terrifying.

Could I make love to this woman every night? Could I wake up with her every morning? And be happy?

I need to think.

Carefully, I extricate myself from Echo and roll out of bed, reaching into my suitcase and grabbing the first pair of shorts I find. Then I swipe my phone off the nightstand and tiptoe to the balcony.

I've got to get my head on straight.

When I glance at the device, a text Jayci sent in the middle of the night pops up.

I wish you could come over NOW! My aching pussy is sloppy wet. I need you to tongue it until I scream. Then I want to suck the skin off your cock and swallow your hot load before we fuck ourselves raw. Don't you wish you could come over, too? LOL!

I darken the device.

Jayci sexts me like that for booty calls all the time. Normally, I jump, showing up with a smile, a bottle, and condoms. This morning, I don't reply.

I have no interest in her. I'm afraid to admit what that means.

Leaning on the railing, I take in the cool Hawaiian breeze and let out a rough breath. As the sun rises, the gray of the early morning sky gives way to a pale blue with pink clouds. Palms sway. Surf rolls. The resort is quiet and serene.

Why is everything in my head so fucking loud?

I scroll through my phone, ignoring Jayci's message, and dial the only person who can help me.

She answers quickly. "Hayes?"

"Hey, Gramma. How you doing?"

"Fine." But her voice says she's not.

I'm worried. "Liar. You sound sad."

"Rose's funeral is tomorrow." She sighs. "She never married, you know. And she regretted it."

I didn't know. I assumed that, like Liddy, she was a widow. "Does she have any other family coming to the service?"

"Probably not. Her sisters have both passed away. She wasn't close to her nieces and nephews. She was a hard woman to get to know. Always busy with work. She thought there would be time later, kind of like someone else I know."

She means me, and won't she be shocked when I tell her why I'm calling?

"What time is her service? Do you need a car?"

"You don't have to call me a service. I know how to Uber, young man."

I grin. One thing about my grandmother, she's feisty and spry. "Yes, ma'am."

"I'm glad you called. It's nice to hear a friendly voice. It's horrible and heartbreaking not to hear Rose's anymore."

The catch in her words tug at me. Liddy must be lonely, and I feel guilty for being too busy in the last year to see her. I need to rectify that.

"I'm sorry, Gramma."

"Thank you, but I'm just feeling sorry for myself today. It's useless, and I need to stop. How's your week in Hawaii with Echo?"

"Funny you should ask..." I blow out a breath and prepare to admit out loud the truth that sucker-punched me last night. "You were right. There are more to my feelings for Echo than I thought."

Her cackling laugh is a mixture of joy and vindication. "It's about time. She loves you, too, by the way."

Does she? When she gave herself over to me last night, I would have sworn she felt more than sexual curiosity. But in the harsh morning light, I realize that my feelings, while real, aren't actual reality. This may be just a fling to her. I may be just a friend willing to do away with her pesky V-card. And at the end of this week, she might be ready for new sexual adventures—with the man she'll eventually fall for—and tuck me back into the friend zone.

"I don't know."

Liddy scoffs. "I do because I know women. She's been waiting for you to pull your head out of your ass and realize you're perfect for each other."

Has she? "I'm terrified."

"That she'll turn you down? Don't be silly."

That's crossed my mind, but it's not my biggest worry. "No. If she does, I'll apologize for misreading the situation and do my best to repair the damage between us."

Then what? Try to go back to being the best friend a girl could need? Fuck, that sounds like torture…but it's better than doing without Echo altogether.

If I somehow manage, it won't be simple. I'm no expert at love. Hell, I just realized I might be in it. But I'm already sure there's more to falling out of it than merely wishing I could.

Then again, what if Echo really does have feelings for me, too? She gave up the notion of Xavian taking her virginity the minute I volunteered. She's always been the perfect friend, but this week she's somehow morphed into my fantasy. How? And why, if she's not trying to please me?

"You're worried she'll hurt you?" Liddy's tone makes it clear that notion is ridiculous. "Bah."

"Not intentionally. Echo's heart is too big."

"Ah, you're worried you'll hurt her?"

"Yeah." That would kill me. "You said I'm nothing like Dad, but…" Technically, I've never been unfaithful to a girlfriend, but only because I've never felt compelled enough to take one. "He tore Mom apart." Me, too. Watching my mother stifle tears to put on those terrible brave faces and lie to me about why Dad wasn't coming home again was horrible.

And what kind of lover am I that I haven't called—or even thought of—Jayci the whole time I've been in Maui. I just ignored the one message she sent me. Not that we're together or exclusive, but I've been banging her for months. Shouldn't I be missing her at least a little?

"Listen to me, young man. Your father wasn't capable of love."

"I know. And I have his genes."

"You think one of your chromosomes decides whether you're a philandering asshole?" I can practically hear my grandmother rolling her eyes. "Don't be ridiculous. It's about your heart, and you have a kind one. You're nothing like your father. You've always been a sweet boy. Do you remember when you used to pick flowers from the backyard for me?"

Gramma kept a big garden out back, and when I spent summers with her, I'd pluck her prettiest blooms and give them to her because she'd always smile as she put them in a big vase on the kitchen table so she could ooh and aah. The memory makes me wince. "Yeah, sorry about that. I know those flowers were your pride and joy."

"Nonsense. More always bloomed, and I loved you bringing them to me. Why did you pick them for me? Because you wanted me to be happy, right?"

"Of course." In some ways, Gramma Liddy was more like a mother to me than my own.

"Because you care about others. Your father, on the other hand, got a thrill out of riding his bike through my garden to kill the flowers because he enjoyed everyone else's misery. He took particular delight in breaking your mother's heart over and over because she suffered horribly and was too weak to stop him."

I can't argue with that. "But being a good kid is no indication that I'd be a good husband."

God, am I even thinking about that kind of commitment with Echo?

"I see you're determined to play devil's advocate. You get that from me, by the way." She laughs wryly.

I probably do. "Habit."

"How about this? Hypothetically, remove sex from the equation."

We're talking about *that* now? "Gramma—"

"Don't be embarrassed. Sex is natural. After all, you wouldn't be here if I'd never had it. But sex isn't relevant to this discussion."

I wince. It's also not comfortable hearing about my grandparents getting frisky or whatever they called it back then. "What's your point?"

"I'm getting there. And don't give me the tripe that, because you're a man, not thinking about sex is impossible."

Maybe not impossible, but deeply, highly, incredibly difficult. Still… "You don't understand."

She sighs noisily. "Echo may not be a supermodel, but she's a cute girl. Certainly, you find *something* attractive about her. Whatever it is, you can build from there. After all, people fall in love not with the body, but with the soul."

"Gramma, Echo is beautiful. We have great chemistry. Sex—if we have it—isn't going to be the problem."

"You two haven't yet?"

"She's been waiting for someone special. I don't know if that's me."

"It is. Hear me out. How long has Echo been your closest friend?"

"Almost eighteen years."

It's crazy that we've been besties that long. Sometimes it seems like another lifetime ago that we were two kids sitting in the elementary school's front office, both on our first day in a new place. And sometimes I'd swear it was last week. Echo said hello first. She offered me a Red

Vine, then she asked me where I'd moved from and why I talked funny. I've since lost my Boston accent but thankfully kept the friend.

"You help each other."

I shrug. "That's what friends do."

"You protect her."

"Of course. I care what happens to her."

"She's always been there for you."

"Echo is there for everyone. Hell, she's taking a job assisting underprivileged kids."

"Just like you've always been there for her."

"Because she's needed it. The only other people she could count on were her sisters. Now that they're married and they've moved away..."

"You're taking care of her. Why would you do that, Hayes? Ask yourself."

My grandmother is backing me into a corner. The mental space is getting tight. I don't like it.

"That doesn't mean I'm in love with her." *Does it?*

"Why do you spend so much time with Echo? Why do you take her camping when you go with your guy friends? Why did you bring her to Hawaii?"

"I like being with her. She's fun. She's chill. She's sweet. She's easy to talk to." She's also sexy as fuck and blows my doors off every time I kiss her.

Are you sure you're not in love?

"Uh-huh. And why did you go with Echo to her middle sister's wedding in Vegas when I know it was a terrible time to pry yourself away from work? And why did you stay away from both the Black Jack tables and the strippers, two of your father's favorites?"

"Because she didn't want to go alone." *And because you didn't want to leave her side.*

"Do you feel half that protective or invested in the last girl you took to bed?"

"Gramma..." I huff.

But I'm hiding behind indignation because she's got a point...

"Answer me."

"No."

"The last five put together?"

I sigh. "No."

"If you could only talk to one woman for the rest of your life?"

There's the unavoidable, crucial question…and the shocking answer that punches me in the gut.

I stare out at the rolling ocean, mute. Then I close my eyes. "I'd pick Echo. God, I'm a dumb ass."

"For not seeing that you're in love with her, too? Totally. At least you're willing to admit it. The good news is, now that you know, you can fix it."

I swallow hard. "What if I suck at being faithful?"

"Hayes, you love her too much to stray. And the fact you're worried puts you light years ahead of your father. Trust me. Go grab your girl and make her yours. You two will be so happy together. And the first wedding invitation you mail better be addressed to me."

"She's not even my girlfriend yet."

"An hour and some groveling will fix that. Trust me."

I hope she's right. But if I'm going to tell Echo how I feel, I have to do it the right way. I can't blurt this. I can't half-ass it. She can't think it has anything to do with her request to lose her V-card, either. She can't feel less than totally special. She has to believe I'm hers.

Liddy and I ring off, and I make a mental note to check in with her after Rose's funeral. For now, my first order of business? I pull up Jayci's message. When I reread it, I frown. In the past, that would have kickstarted my libido into overdrive. Now it leaves me feeling somewhere between unmoved and needing a shower. I tap back a message to her.

I've done some thinking over the past few days. I don't think we're suited for each other, and I won't be coming by anymore. You deserve someone who cares about you, and that's not me. Take care.

An instant later, I get a message back. **I didn't need or want you to care about me. I just wanted your cock. But whatever. Fuck off.**

If that's the way she feels, cool. I'm moving on. Moving forward—with Echo.

Suddenly, I've got an idea to show her exactly how I feel. Tonight can't come soon enough.

* * * *

After I make a few phone calls from the balcony, another half hour has passed. I push back into our suite to discover Echo gone. On the table near the sofa, I spot a note she jotted.

Your calls looked intense. I'm bringing back java and a bite. How do you feel about surfing today?

E

I set down the note with a smile. I'll probably make an idiot out of myself with a surfboard, but what the hell? I'll have more time with Echo...and she'll probably be in another bikini designed to make my tongue drag the ground after her. We're already in paradise. She doesn't sound upset about anything that went down last night.

After I finish wrapping my head around what's in my heart, today should be good.

A knock on the door sends me running. Echo probably has her hands full, so I pull it open. But she isn't the person standing in my doorway.

"X, man. Come on in." I step back, taking in his frown. "How are you doing?"

He follows me. "I'm okay. You?"

"Good."

"Where's E?"

"She'll be right back."

Xavian sends me a sly grin. "So how did last night go? Could you actually keep your hands off of her? And your dick out of her?"

None of his business. "It was fine. What happened with your new family? Curiosity satisfied? Ready to be the lone wolf again?"

"About that..." Xavian grimaces. "I'm staying with them."

"For the rest of the week?"

He shakes his head. "For the foreseeable future. I'm moving here."

Is he serious? "To Maui? To be with strangers you met yesterday?"

"To a fucking gorgeous place with people I feel like I've known all my life."

"As opposed to the people you actually have?"

"Don't get me wrong, man. You, E, Graham, Kella, and Maryam are the most solid friends I could ask for. If it wasn't for you all, after my mom died I would have either driven my car into an embankment or bit a bullet. I felt so alone. I know I wasn't, but none of you could relate to the hell I was going through. And I'm glad. I wouldn't wish that kind of loss on anyone. You all have other family to fall back on. Me? There's always been a giant hole where my father should have been. I wondered why he rejected me before I was even born. When I'd ask, my mother would only say we were better off without my sperm donor. She took his identity to her fucking grave... I've never celebrated a Father's Day. I can't fill out a medical history form about the paternal side of my family. And unless it was some other kid I went to school with, no one ever so much as tossed a ball with me. Now that I have siblings who want to patch together a family as much as I do, don't fucking judge me."

There's the familiar chip on X's shoulder. We've all seen and felt it. And I get where he's coming from, even if I don't totally understand. "Hey, that's not what's happening here. You're my friend. I'm worried about you. Can you really count on the Reeds?"

"This will sound weird, but after an evening with them I don't feel that gaping hole in my life anymore."

I rear back. That's a lot, coming from X. "Where will you live on the island? Where will you work? What will you do?"

Especially if it doesn't work out.

"Bethany... Do you remember my sister with the blonde hair?" He smiles. "It still feels weird saying that I have brothers and sisters."

The pretty one with the unusual gray-green eyes? "Yeah."

"Dude, she's a financial genius. She and her husband, Clint, opened a private, boutique investment firm three weeks ago, just after their honeymoon. But his background is in oil and gas, and he didn't go to college, so he'll be in school while studying for the CFP exam. She's already got more business than she can handle alone."

Seriously? "How much is she managing?"

"Nearly a billion dollars. She'll have to turn away clients if she doesn't get help fast."

"Holy shit."

"She's good, man. She's shrewd and ballsy. She knows tons of movers and shakers. I appreciate you helping me get a job, but if I stayed in LA as your wingman, I'd start at the bottom and do years of menial shit before anyone took off the training wheels. With Bethany, I can make a difference right now. We talked about it last night. We worked through a few clients' files together, like an audition. I made suggestions. We discussed everything, then jointly developed a strategy. The market is about to close. Together, we've made those three clients close to six figures *each* today."

"Wow." If that's true, it sounds like a hell of an opportunity, and I would never want to hold him back. "That's insane."

"Right? I can learn a ton from her. She's been working in the financial sector since earning her MBA from Harvard at twenty."

It's hard not to be impressed by that. "Then, yeah. It sounds like a hell of an opportunity you shouldn't pass up. Does she know you haven't taken the CFP exam yet?"

He nods. "Last night, I registered to take it in August. Bethany says she'll help me study. She needs me to get up to speed before the baby comes. Clint won't be ready to fly solo by then, and she's panicked."

With good reason. "You're one hundred percent sure you want to do this?"

"Ninety-five. I know it's a really fast decision, but I've thought it through a few times in my head. The only thing keeping me in LA is my friends. I won't miss my crappy apartment. And even if I get a crappy apartment on the island? Dude, I'll be in Maui. I'll go from having no family to having six siblings, along with a niece, three nephews, and more on the way. And I think I'll make some cool friends, like Noah Weston's younger brother, Trace, and his fiancée, Masey. Evan's best friend, Sebastian, is a lot like me—completely sarcastic. We had a ton in common." X falls quiet. "My gut tells me this is the right move. But I'm going to fucking miss all of you back home."

"It will be weird as hell without you around. We'll miss you, too." He stands, and we exchange a bro hug, complete with back slaps.

"Thanks for understanding. You can visit me anytime, you know."

"I appreciate that. I admit, I wouldn't mind coming back here."

Xavian settles into his chair again, then frowns. "The other reason I came is for E. If last night was merely 'fine,' then you didn't pop her cherry. I gave you a night to see if you'd change your mind about that. Since you didn't, I'm here to fulfill my promise to her. She wants to feel like a woman—at least for a night. I can give her that."

X might be trying to keep his word, but his persistence about getting into Echo's panties pisses me off. "You're not touching her."

"If you're not going to man up, then you don't get a say. It's her choice."

"What I've got going with Echo is none of your business. You will not fucking touch her, X. Not tonight. Not this week. Not ever. Drop it."

Brow raised, he sends me a cutting stare. "Or what? I'm not breaking my promise to her without a good reason. You being delusional enough to think you know better than Echo how to live her life isn't it."

I lunge out of my seat and grab the sides of his chair, mostly to keep myself from punching him. "If you touch her, I will beat you senseless. And we can't be friends anymore."

In the heat of the moment, the threat slips out. But I'm dead serious.

Xavian looks at me like he has no idea who I am. Honestly, I don't know this side of me, either. Until Echo, I've never been jealous. "Wow. What a douche. Echo has feelings for you. You keep saying you're doing what's best for her, but you're full of shit." He pushes me away and stands. "I know you're still fucking Jayci. Her roommate told me you did her the night before we left—loudly. So I guess it's okay for you to have your something-something, but you'll *lie* to Echo to keep her sweet and virginal so that when you finally run out of Jaycis, Lindsays, Brittanys, and Angelas to bone you'll have your bestie as a backup."

"That's not what's happening."

"Then what is?"

I can't tell Xavian that I think I'm in love with Echo before I tell her myself. He's not exactly a fortress when it comes to keeping secrets.

"You know I'm right," he spits. "E is no one's plan B. Don't you dare treat her like that! At least I leveled with her. I told her if she wanted romance, I wasn't her guy. But she said she just wanted to fuck—"

"No!" I snarl in his face, my blood pressure soaring.

I can't picture him touching her without losing my damn mind.

"Why? You're never going to treat her like more than a pal. So let her fucking get over you."

"With you?"

"With someone she trusts who won't break her heart." Xavian glares at me with those piercing eyes, shaking his head. "But you already did. Good job," he says snidely. "By the way, I'm offering E the key to my room down the hall or a place in my bed at the Westons' for the rest of the week. After I tell her what you're really up to, I'll let her decide which she'd rather have. Enjoy being alone, you selfish bastard. You deserve it."

With a shake of his head, Xavian lunges for the door and tosses it wide open, the solid wooden surface banging loudly against the door stop as he stomps into the breezeway, then disappears around the corner.

"Fuck," I mutter under my breath.

I have to find Echo now…before he does.

Chapter Eight

Echo doesn't answer her phone. I leave voice mails practically begging her to call me.

Thirty minutes turn into an hour. Then two. My hope that Xavian didn't get to her first evaporates.

What else is he doing to her?

Fuck.

Has he told Echo that I don't have feelings for her? That I never intended to make love to her? That she should settle for a night with him instead? Is he already taking off her clothes? Getting her horizontal? Working his way inside her? Those possibilities have me pacing. He won't value her the way she deserves. She'll regret him.

I will, too. She's mine…even if I haven't yet confessed to her how I feel.

Seeing her things scattered around the room makes me miss her. Looking at the sofa she lay on last night while I plied kisses to her naked body makes me ache. Remembering the pleasure of Echo's hair in my fists as she slid my cock into her mouth…and wondering if she's doing the same to Xavian right now because he insists I feel an aloofness I'm not sure I ever did makes me in-fucking-sane.

By noon, it's obvious she's not coming back soon. I can't just sit here. I need to stop what-ifing and find her.

I search the property, just in case, but it's raining, so it's easy to see she's not at any of the virtually empty pools or on the deserted beach. She's not in Xavian's room, either. No one is. She's gone. I don't know where she is or when she's coming back…or if she'll even be speaking to me next time I see her.

Panic sets in. My chances with her slip away with every passing tick of the clock.

Desperate, I grab the rental car keys and head toward the only other place she might be. My head hurts like a bitch because I haven't had food or coffee yet, and my stress level is off the charts.

As I jet down the damp, winding road, it hits me that I'm not half as worried about Echo giving her virginity to someone else as I am about her being so angry that I lied to her—even if I meant well—that she'll cut me out of her life. Ironic, right? On the day I realize I'm in love with her, she may decide she doesn't need a manipulative best friend who she's convinced will never take her seriously as a lover.

I could blame Xavian for filling Echo's head with bullshit. But if anyone deserves the blame, it's me. I was too self-absorbed, too afraid, and too busy indulging in all the easy ass to see the right woman was in front of me. At the thought of not being able to pick up the phone to hear Echo's soft, quirky voice or being able to see her adorable dimpled smile every day, I nearly lose my shit. A thousand Jaycis, Lindsays, Brittanys, and Angelas put together can't replace my one perfect Echo.

Why was I so fucking stupid that I didn't spend all my time and give my whole heart to the woman who deserves it most?

By the time I reach the Sunshine Coast Bed-and-Breakfast, the rain thankfully pauses. Keeley says something to the crowd of guests gathering for yoga by the ocean, then crosses the lawn to me with a frown.

"Hayes? What brings you here?"

"Hi. Have you seen Xavian and Echo today?"

She shakes her head. "He spent the night at Harlow and Noah's place. I wouldn't be surprised if he's with Bethany and Clint now, but I don't know for sure. You think Echo is with him? You look upset. Are you all right?"

No, and I don't know where to go from here. "Would anyone else know where to find them?"

"Um…hang here for a minute." She runs back to the waiting guests, grabs her phone, and dashes off a quick text. Then she turns back to me, holding up a finger. Her phone lights up, and she scans it, then sends me a thumbs up and a smile.

What the devil does that mean? She knows where they are? Is she coming back to tell me?

Apparently not. She starts some of the flute-based yoga music she played the other day and warms up with the small crowd following her. Eleanor appears on the lanai with the baby. Is she coming with information about Xavian and Echo? When she sits and plays with the infant, making peekaboo faces and laughing, I guess not.

Finally, a tall stranger, dressed like a *GQ* model, complete with swagger, emerges from the back of the house. He waves at Eleanor, pauses to rub Kailani's head, then heads straight for me. Who the fuck is this guy?

I swallow as he approaches, hand outstretched. "Sebastian Shaw."

The sarcastic guy Xavian mentioned earlier. Is he coming to deliver a Dear John message on Echo's behalf? "Hayes Elliot."

"You're wondering why I'm here. You met Evan Cook yesterday, right? He's my boss and best friend."

And one of X's newfound brothers. "Yeah. Do you know where to find Xavian or Echo?"

"No. I've been here working on a project that… Well, let's just put it this way. Nothing good comes when you sleep with the enemy." He gives me an acidic, self-deprecating smile. "But that's not your issue. I can help you find them. Xavian and I knocked back a few beers last night. He said you're all friends?"

"Yeah. We've been super-tight." Or we were until this week.

"But something happened?"

I nod and hope it's enough. I don't want to expend the time or humiliation explaining that everything blew up because I handled my feelings so horribly.

"Look, I know you don't know me, but I'm willing to listen—"

"I appreciate that." The guy means well, but I don't have time for this shit. "But I've got everything under control."

"Sure, you do. That's why you're here asking strangers where to find your closest pals and looking half ready to crawl out of your skin." He claps me on the shoulder. "I'll leave you to it."

Sebastian *is* a sarcastic fucker.

When he turns away, I growl under my breath. Damn it, he's the only one who can help me right now. My pride has to take a back seat. "Wait. Please. I need to find Echo. She's probably with Xavian. I have to talk to her."

He crosses his arms over his chest and gives me a considering once-over. "Tell me the situation, and I'll see what I can do."

What the fuck? I'm not thrilled about word-vomiting all my personal shit, but the way he's looking at me tells me he won't move a muscle unless I start talking. "In a nutshell? I've been an idiot about my feelings for Echo, and I need to tell her before Xavian convinces her otherwise. He's a good friend, but…she's always been my closest. X doesn't love her. He doesn't even want her. So I can't let her make a mistake with him."

Sebastian stares at me for such a long time, I'm half convinced he'll tell me to take my boo-hoo problems somewhere else and get out of his face. Instead, he sighs. "Sorry to hear that, man. I've kind of been in this situation."

Of all the things he could have said, I didn't expect that. "Seriously?"

"Not exactly the same, but enough to know how you feel. Um, Evan told you he was widowed before he married Nia?"

"He mentioned that." I'm still shocked that a guy barely thirty had to bury his pregnant wife. "It sounds tragic."

"For everyone. He didn't love Becca." Sebastian blows out a breath. "I did."

Wait…what? "You were in love with your best friend's wife? Whoa. Were you two…" The question slips out before I realize it's none of my business.

"No. I would never have betrayed Evan like that. But he knows now that I loved her. We've talked. The one thing I can tell you? We all would have been less miserable if we'd been honest with ourselves and each other."

"I'm trying to. That's what I want to talk to Echo about. But I can't fucking find her so I can ask her to listen."

Sebastian nods slowly, then reaches for his phone. He shoots off a text, and gets one back quickly. "Go back to the hotel."

"And do what? Echo isn't there."

"Wait. When she shows up, if she's willing to talk, shelve your pride. Treat tonight like it's your first—and last—chance to convince her to choose you. Take it from the guy who buried the woman he loved without ever telling her how he felt. Maybe the truth would have ruined everything. And maybe it wouldn't have changed anything. I'll never know. What I did learn? Regret is bitter, and it lasts forever."

* * * *

By eight o'clock that night, it's a wonder I haven't worn holes in the hotel room's dark, utilitarian carpet with my pacing. Finally, I hear the click of the latch. The door slowly opens.

Echo steps in. She looks wary.

She's been crying.

My knees nearly go out from under me. I did this to her, and I feel fucking horrible. What if she can't forgive me? "Shortcake...I'm so sorry."

She shakes her head, then looks past me, taking in the rest of the room with a confused furrow of her brows. Since I've been consumed by dread that she isn't coming back, I'd half forgotten about the rose petals scattered across the pristine white comforter on our bed and the champagne chilling next to the nightstand.

"What's this?" She sounds shocked and...something else. Horrified?

"My attempt to seduce you." I cross the room to her, but stop short. I want to touch Echo, but I need to find out where her head is. "I guess Xavian told you I had no intention of making love to you."

She nods, arms wrapped around herself as if she needs a hug and doesn't trust me to give it to her. "He did."

Goddamn it, I wish he would have let me confess my own screw-ups, but I understand why he didn't. "I'm sorry for lying to you. You wanted to lose your virginity with someone who would make it good for you, and I took that decision away. It wasn't fair."

"So why did you?"

"When Xavian first let it slip that he intended to take you to bed, I told myself I couldn't let you because you would regret it. He's a man whore. He doesn't love you..." I blow out a breath. "And I thought I could save you."

That only seems to make Echo unhappier since tears mist her big eyes. "My decision must have seemed impulsive to you. I know you meant well, and I appreciate you trying to help me, but—"

"I was an idiot. And an asshole. The truth is, I didn't want Xavian touching you."

"But you weren't willing to, either." She scans the romantic scene I staged and cringes. "Until tonight, I guess. But I don't want your pity, especially not this kind."

"What? No! That's not—"

"You don't have to try and make me feel better. You've made your point. We're friends. Just friends. And what I wanted went way beyond that."

"Hang on." I approach slowly and hold out my hand, hoping like fuck she'll take it. "Echo, I just didn't—"

"Want me. I know. And I'm the one who's sorry, string bean." She shies away with a sniffle. "I haven't been a very good friend."

What the hell is she talking about? "No, you've always been the most loyal, caring, kind, positive—"

"I've been lying to you about my feelings since I was a freshman in high school. That's how long I've been in love with you."

Shock drops the bottom out of my stomach. Is she serious? "You've felt this way for eight years?"

She nods, her expression desolate as more tears fall. "I was fourteen when I first realized it. I felt so lucky that the cutest sophomore boy was my best friend. I remember putting on my prettiest dress the first Thursday in December, when tickets to the Winter Formal finally went up for sale. I saw you buy a pair during lunch. Then you walked up to me, looking so excited. My stomach flipped and my heart pounded. I was sure you were going to ask me. But you invited Kaitlyn instead."

I barely remember that girl...except that we made out after the dance, and I got my hands on her tits.

"You took Allie to Spring Fling. You asked Jasmine to the End-of-School bash. And you spent all summer having sex with Dakota." She's sobbing now.

Shit. I've hurt her so much. I want to touch and comfort her, but I have no right. I feel like a heel for never noticing her feelings.

"Shortcake, I had no idea..." I reach for Echo.

She shrugs me off. "Because I didn't want you to. But it hurt to hear you talk about other girls all the time, especially what you did with them."

I did talk. Hell, it probably sounded like bragging. I didn't think Echo noticed. Or cared.

No, you didn't think at all, dumb ass.

"I kept everything to myself because I didn't want to be one of those clingy girls you shed. I couldn't stand the thought of not being around you. And I couldn't stop hoping you'd finally see me. But you didn't." Her voice tells me it was crushing. "College was pretty much a rinse and repeat."

I had no clue. All those years...

"Is that why you chose Xavian to take you to bed? To see if it would hurt me? So I could know how you felt?"

"No. It was my last-ditch effort to see if who I did mattered to you. If you'd be...jealous. X kept insisting you would."

"He was right. I was jealous as hell."

"Because I tricked you into it. Otherwise, you would have never thought about me as more than a friend. I wanted you to see me so badly for once…" Pain twists her face. "So when I begged Xavian to help, he agreed."

My eyes narrow. "Help you how?"

"He started by picking out my clothes for two weeks."

"All those dresses and bikinis?" The ones that had me salivating, like the short, sunny yellow breast-hugging shift she's wearing right now? "They were his idea?"

She nods miserably. "We went shopping. He chose everything, down to the lingerie."

I should have guessed, and the fact he's probably seen her in everything designed to tempt me shreds my guts. "What about the white nightie I could see through once your hair dampened it?"

"That, too. All of it."

"Fuck." I'm going to threaten Xavian if he even thinks about Echo as a woman again.

"I asked him how to drive you crazy, and he coached me on what to do and what to say. I thought I was ready for whatever happened." She winces. "The night we arrived in Hawaii, I had to act upset, but I was thrilled to hear you'd intentionally prevented him from spending the night with me when I'd supposedly planned to give him my virginity."

Supposedly? "You weren't going to?"

"Of course not. I never had any intention of letting him touch me. I only wanted to know if the possibility he might would matter. Instead, I got impatient and I kissed you. I was horrified that I'd thrown myself at you, and I ran. And like the amazing friend you are, you found me, calmed me, took me back to our room, and forgave me. I should have stopped hoping then…but I felt a spark during that kiss."

"Oh, it was more than a spark, shortcake."

"You felt it, too?" She's shocked.

"Yeah. It blindsided me."

A soft flush steals up her cheeks. "After that kiss, I couldn't stop aching."

And like a flaming idiot, instead of wrapping her in my arms and taking her to bed, I tried to figure it out. Dissect it. I kept her waiting and wanting. Worrying and wondering. No, I didn't know she had some ploy up her sleeve, but since I know Echo I should have guessed. Her behavior didn't add up. My only excuse? I hadn't thought of her in *that* way before, so I was slow to catch on. But I'm all in now. Echo is someone I can see myself loving, not just for tonight or this week—but for years.

For forever.

I hope I haven't killed what's between us. She's being honest about her feelings now—and I'm glad—but her face is closing up. How do I prove that my blindness had nothing to do with her, just my idiocy? How can I make her happy?

"But it was a stupid idea to think that friendship could translate into more simply because I ran around in a bikini or two." Her voice warbles. "I'm sorry I tried to manipulate you. I hope our friendship will recover someday. I'll get my stuff and move down the hall to Xavian's room. Enjoy the rest of your vacation."

She lowers her head and makes a beeline for her suitcase, but not before more tears fall down her cheeks. Then her words register. She's leaving?

Hell no.

I hustle behind her and grab her arm, wrapping my own around her waist and bringing her against me, then settle my lips on her ear. "It wasn't a stupid idea, and I don't want you to go."

Echo sends a cautious glance over her shoulder. Our faces are inches apart. The hope in her wide eyes nearly kills me. "What are you saying?"

"Stay, shortcake. I want you. I need to show you how much."

Slowly, Echo turns in my arms. My sense of relief is dizzying when she lets me bring her closer. But before I can kiss her, she stops me. "Are you saying you're willing to sleep with me?"

"Willing to? Try dying to. I woke up this morning and realized I'm crazy about you—and not merely as a friend. I've probably felt this way for a long time, and I was too blind to see it. I—"

"You don't have to say that to make me feel better. I know you and Jayci are...together and—"

"Not anymore. Listen to me, Echo. I love you."

Her lips part on a soft gasp. "No. You're just saying that."

"I'm not, shortcake. I've never said those words to Jayci—or any other woman I've been with—so I'm not blurting BS to make you feel better. You've opened my eyes, and I want you to know what's in my heart. Jayci isn't important to me. None of those girls were. But you were always beside me. Now let me be here with you."

Echo searches my eyes. A duo of fresh tears falls down her cheeks.

"You always have been."

"Not in the way I should have. How did you stay such an amazingly loyal, wonderful friend when I kept hurting you?"

"Because I love you. And I kept hoping that, one day, you'd love me, too."

"I do," I assure her in a fierce whisper as I cup her face in my hands. "I love you more than I realized. More than you know. More than I can tell you with a few words. If you still want me, I won't hold back from showing you how much. And we'll never let the Jaycis and the Xavians of the world come between us again."

Chapter Nine

Echo

If I still want him? I'd say that Hayes can't possibly be serious, but the masculine angles of his face I've memorized because I've stared at them a million times says he is.

"After everything, you're really asking if I want you? Hayes, I have since I was old enough to understand what that even meant. I don't need experience with anyone else to know I always will."

"Shortcake…" He sounds choked and humbled, like this moment means everything to him, the way it does to me. Is that possible?

His stare fastens on mine again, his eyes now dark with desire. Yes, it is. And it's real.

Hayes has always been intense, doing everything with determination and purpose. His expression now tells me he intends to make love to me with that same zeal and fervor.

I gulp and shiver because there's nothing to be nervous about. My fantasy of being the woman Hayes Elliot falls for is finally coming true.

A smile takes my face hostage, curling up my lips with abandon. We should probably talk more, mutually agree that our friendship comes first, no matter what. But there's no need to question that. I know it does. Just like Hayes knows I've waited a half a lifetime for him to want me back.

I launch myself against him, wrapping my arms and legs around his muscled shoulders and narrow hips before planting my lips on his with a moan. He stumbles back for an unsteady moment, groping for balance. But Hayes is athletic. He's mastered many sports over the last decade, so it doesn't take him long to find his footing. The instant he does, he takes my mouth, opening his lips over mine.

His kiss turns ruthless and demanding. Against my heart, his pounds. When I rock my hips, desperate for the friction I need to ease the ache only he's ever made me feel, he's as hard as steel. And when I claw at his shoulders, Hayes grips my ass in his palms, his fingers biting into me as he strokes himself against my pussy with a groan.

It's not enough.

He falls back to the bed with a frantic curse. I tumble on top of him, straddling his hips as our arms and legs tangle. He melds his mouth to mine again. I open my lips and my thighs wider, inviting him deeper and shamelessly rubbing myself against him.

Please, please…lift my skirt, unzip your shorts, and end my years of aching need.

As if he hears my silent pleading, Hayes rolls me to my back, diving deeper into our kiss and drowning me in his masculine taste. He's like spice on my tongue. Potent. Intoxicating. Addictive. But he's so much better than my fantasies because he's so incredibly real.

This close to him, I feel dizzy. Euphoric. My thoughts stop. My body takes over, my heart leading the way.

He slides a spaghetti strap down my arm, baring my shoulder, along with the tan lines from my bikini. I hold my breath as he does the same with the other. Only a few tiny buttons hold my dress in place and conceal my breasts from his hungry stare.

He pauses, his stare drilling into mine. I'm afraid to blink in case this is a vivid dream. But Hayes's expression is too penetrating to be anything but honest.

He reaches for the top button on my dress. "You sure about this?"

My heart kicks into overdrive. "Positive."

"Shortcake, it's okay if you're not ready. We don't have to do this until I make it up to you. I'll be patient. The most important thing to me is earning your trust and making you happy."

That's sweet but… "I've already waited forever. So if you're suggesting we wait longer, that will make me *very* unhappy." But what about him? "Unless you need time to get used to the idea that I'm more than your friend and—"

"I don't. I'm down with it. All I want is you, preferably naked and smiling."

A wave of heat washes over me as I nod. "Then hurry."

"Yes, ma'am." He plows through the buttons on the front of my dress, his fingers a rapid-fire blur as he starts at my cleavage and doesn't stop until the fastenings end at my waist.

The two sides of my bodice part, and he peels them away from my body. Since I'm not wearing a bra, my breasts bounce free. My erect nipples point straight at him, silently begging for his touch.

He groans long and low. "Oh, fuck."

My cheeks heat with giddy excitement. "They're not new. You saw them last night."

"Because you dropped your dress for me. Today, I'm unwrapping you like the special gift you are." He cradles one of my breasts in his big palm, sliding his thumb over the tip, pinging desire through my body. "You're even more beautiful tonight."

That compliment shouldn't melt me, but I close my eyes, savor his touch, and give myself over to him. "You don't know how many times I've imagined you doing this to me."

"Tell me," he breathes on my neck.

I shiver. My ache grows. "So many it's embarrassing."

His sexy groan rumbles against my ear. "I love hearing that you touched yourself to thoughts of me. Next time you start fantasizing, whisper every tiny, dirty detail to me. I'll give you everything you want—anytime, anywhere, and any way you want it."

My breath hitches. Is he trying to steal my sanity before I give him my virginity?

"Take off your shirt." I grab at his tee and yank it impatiently up his torso.

Hayes helps me along, sitting up and reaching behind his neck to jerk the garment over his head. When he tosses it across the room, I gasp.

I've seen his naked torso dozens of times—at the pool, at the soccer pitch, hanging out while watching movies…last night when I had my mouth on his cock. Knowing I can touch him right now and that he'll welcome my fingers on his skin? Knowing he's *mine?* It's a fantasy come true.

Suddenly, I can't keep my hands off my best friend's body. I skim my fingertips over his wide shoulders, tracing their hard curves before setting my palms on the solid bulges of his pecs. His exhalations turn rougher when I drag my thumbs across his nipples the way he did to mine. Then he closes his eyes, frowning like he's fighting to restrain the urge to climb all over me.

I flit my lips up his strong neck, lingering over his thudding pulse, and guide his hands back to my breasts. "Don't hold back for me."

"Echo, I'm trying to take this slow. You're killing my good intentions."

"Glad to hear it." I gather my too-short skirt in my hands and tug it up.

Xavian insisted these dresses make my legs look amazing. I've felt self-conscious wearing flounces and ruffles that end a scant couple of inches below my underwear, but seeing Hayes visually devour me and being with him here now… It's been worth it.

I yank the dress over my head and fling it across the room. That leaves me wearing only a tiny pair of blush pink panties, held up by a ridiculously thin strip of lace clinging to each hip. Hayes's stare climbs up my thighs, traces those bands of lace, before grazing the indention of my waist, dipping to my belly button…then dropping to focus between my legs. His eyes narrow and darken.

The front panel of these nearly nonexistent panties is completely see-through. It clings wetly to my bare, Xavian-swore-Hayes-would-love-it-waxed pussy. Hayes's hot stare tells me Xavian was right.

My pulse jumps. My womb clenches. My ache sharpens. His cock swells, getting even harder. He swallows like he's digging even deeper for control.

"Echo." He murmurs my name like a benediction. "Damn, you're beautiful."

I pull the pins from my hair, and the heavy bun coiled on top of my head falls loose and free, the ends curling under my elbows and brushing the ticklish skin just above my panties. "You make me feel that way."

Hayes thrusts his fingers into my hair and fists the strands, using his grip to pull me in for a kiss. The instant our mouths merge and our bare chests meet, I melt against him, clutching him tighter with a groan and losing myself in the moment. It's everything I've dreamed of—and more. In my forbidden thoughts, Hayes merely wanted me. But knowing he loves me, too? I can't wait to give him my all.

I open wider and take more of his kiss. He tosses me onto my back and rolls on top of me, sliding his hips between my legs and rocking against me. I swoon. God, I want him more than I thought I could ever want any man.

"Hayes," I pant between kisses, planting my feet on the mattress, lifting to meet every downward thrust of his hips.

His mouth trails up my neck. His teeth nip at my lobe. He's trying to consume me, so he doesn't answer. Not that I'm surprised. When Hayes concentrates on something, his focus is absolute. That's the case as he kisses his way across my shoulders, past my collarbones, and heads straight for my nipples. And just like yesterday, when he takes one in his mouth, pleasure feels like a live wire sizzling my whole body. I'm struggling to process those sensations when his fingers find their way into my panties, and he settles a pair of fingers over my sensitive clit.

Slowly, torturously, he rubs me. My back arches. My legs go taut. I cry out. Ecstasy threatens to overtake me, erasing everything except my love for Hayes.

"Look at you..." he breathes against my breasts. "So trembling and rosy, willing to surrender every part of yourself to me."

"I've saved it all for you," I gasp.

"I know, shortcake. I'm so fucking lucky. I'm going to treasure every bit while I worship you. When I'm done, you'll never doubt again how much I want you. Or how much I love you."

At those words, I shiver. Then he takes my nipples—one after the other—into his mouth while his fingers work me mercilessly. The ache is more than I can bear. The closer he brings me to the edge, the more I shudder and plead. The harder I pant. The more desperately I need.

"Hayes! Please. Now."

He strips off my panties and runs his fingertips slowly, reverently over the bare pad of my pussy, despite the fact I'm a shaking, pleading mass of arousal. I love the way he looks at me when he's got his hands on me, like I'm his wonderful everything. But he's not undressing himself so he can make love to me.

That's not okay.

"You have to stop touching"—my breath hitches when he skims my most sensitive spot—"me. You're tormenting me."

"I am. You're amazing, so soft and swollen. So wet. I love watching you shiver and pant. Just a little more..."

"Now!" I shove him to his back and attack the button at his waistband.

A smile plays at Hayes's lips. "Eager much?"

Isn't he? Maybe not yet. I haven't had the chance to get my hands on him. Though the tables are turned, my body hums as if his fingers still flirt between my legs and his tongue still grazes the hard tips of my breasts. It's driving me insane. But I'm dying to excite him just as much.

I yank down his zipper and tug his shorts off. Then I stare at his cock—long and thick with a rigid staff and a head purple with need. I swallow, and my mouth goes dry.

"What if I do this?" I whisper as I wrap my hand around his cock, pumping him slowly, moving above him to settle my mouth on his nipples.

"Fuck," he groans, seeming to melt into the mattress. "The feel of your hand on me... Oh, damn."

"Eager now?"

"Shortcake, I've been eager since I realized I was in love with you." His breaths are labored. "I just want you to be ready so it doesn't hurt. I want it to be good for you."

Every time I think I can't love Hayes more, he says something wonderful that proves me wrong. "I know you, string bean. You'll do everything you can for me. You always have."

He rolls me to my back with a nod, brushing my hair from my face. "I always will."

Then he reaches for a condom. I press a hand to his chest. "You don't need that. I'm on the pill."

Hayes freezes. "Since when?"

I've shocked him. He thought he knew everything about me... "Since last month, when you surprised me with this trip."

"Shortcake..." He swallows, drilling down into my eyes. "I've never not worn a condom with someone. I've been tested recently. I'm clean. But I'll glove up if it will make you feel safer."

Slowly, I shake my head. "I never want anything between us again."

He lowers his hand. "Same. I want to be as close to you as I can."

Then there's nothing left to say until he settles his body over mine and kisses me with reverence. Before Hayes has even made love to me, I already know I'll be his forever.

Our kiss lingers, deepens, turns more urgent. I grip his shoulders. He settles his hands on my hips. I spread my legs to him. He slides between them. I lift in welcome. He aligns the head of his hard shaft against me. I hold my breath.

Then he pauses, his exhalations against my mouth uneven and rapid. "Ready?"

"I have been for years."

His face softens as he presses our foreheads together for a solemn moment, then looks at me again. "I love you."

"I love you. No more stalling."

He winces. "I don't want to hurt you."

"The only way you can do that is if you friend-zone me again."

"That's not possible anymore. You're mine now."

He fits his lips over mine, plumbing the depths of my mouth as he thrusts into me with an urgent press of his hips and tunnels deep with one sure stroke. I gasp, both at the tinge of discomfort and the new sensation of every inch of Hayes Elliot filling me.

Oh, my god. The two of us are one now.

"Shortcake," he groans, gruff and gravelly. "Jesus, you feel good. You okay?"

"Yes."

He breathes hard, struggling to control himself when he cups my face. "Still hurting?"

"A little." Maybe more than that, but I know it won't last long. Hayes won't let it.

He frowns. "Let me make you feel good."

I have no idea what he's planning until he grabs a pillow from the bed, shoves it under my hips, then eases back, almost withdrawing.

Panic bites at me. "Don't stop."

"Never." Between us, he settles a thumb over my clit and circles the hard bud. A bolt of shocking pleasure shoots through me, settling right where we're joined. Then slowly, he fills me again with a moan that rips from his chest. "Ever."

This time, the pain is nonexistent. Instead, friction fills me with a flurry of tingles, and when he cants his hips forward, pressing even deeper into me, he rubs a spot that has me gasping. My eyes go wide and zip up to his. I grip his shoulders. "Do that again."

He grins. "My pleasure."

Hayes does. The sensations grow. I suck in a shocked breath as more sensations impale me.

"Better?" he asks, sounding strained.

"Hmm… Great."

"Thank god." He surges deep again and again and again, settling into a rhythm that compels me to rock with him.

We move as one, and desire floods every nerve in my body. Desperate to be closer, I kiss my way up his neck to nip at his lips and I wrap my legs around him, silently begging him to never stop.

With every thrust, he scrapes a nerve-filled spot I never knew existed. The ache between my legs coils tighter. Hayes's exhalations become guttural sounds of agonized pleasure. The bed squeaks. Sweat forms at his temples. My whole body tenses, poised on the edge of something amazing. My nails find their way to his shoulders and dig in needy supplication. He doesn't disappoint, just fills me harder and faster.

"You're tightening," he grates out.

"I'm close." So close I can hardly find my breath.

He surges even deeper as if he's never had anything sweeter and he intends to consume me whole. I lose myself in him, to him—for good. "Oh…yes!"

Ruthlessly, he settles his thumb over my clit again. With the other hand, he digs his fingers into my hair and forces me to look into his eyes as he shoves inside me, pervading every inch of my body.

"Echo." His dark eyes delve into mine.

The connection is like nothing I've ever imagined in, even my wildest fantasies. It trips me into the sort of ecstasy I've never, ever felt. I let go, screaming, my pleasure liquid until I'm boneless putty in his hands. Hayes falls into the abyss with me, driving the rapture up another shocking notch with rapid strokes as he crushes me in his possessive embrace.

The pulsing and shuddering seem to last a blissful forever before my brain slowly returns. I open my eyes to find Hayes staring down at me with a love I never dared to believe I'd see on his face.

"Oh, my god. That was…everything, shortcake."

I offer up my lips for a soft kiss as tears of joy sting my eyes. "More than I ever imagined. I love you."

"I love you, too." He thumbs my damp temples with a reverence that propels more tears to fall. "You know you're never getting rid of me now."

"We'll need to leave the bed occasionally to eat, drink, and shower. You have the final mixer on Friday night, right?"

"I'll skip it."

"I might need a break by then." In fact, I fidget because I could use one now. The pleasure is fading into a lovely, mellow glow, but my girl parts are a little tender.

"If you're sore, shortcake, I'll kiss it and make it better," he promises, but his sly grin flattens into something serious. "But I didn't mean this week. I meant for the rest of our lives. You ready for that?"

His question lights me up all the way to my soul. "With you? That's what I've always wanted."

Epilogue

Los Angeles
Sunday, May 20

It was an amazing week in paradise. So much has happened, I can barely believe it.

After Hayes so sweetly plucked my V-card on Tuesday, we barely made it out of bed for days. We managed to tear ourselves away from each other long enough to have dinner with Xavian and his newfound family on Thursday evening. He seemed so happy, and he fits in with the Reed clan as if he was born there. I'm thrilled for him. His decision to stay seemed sudden at first, but I think it was the right one.

On Friday night, Hayes and I spent ten whole minutes at the company's final mixer, just long enough for him to make contact with some of the peers he met last weekend, shake Mr. Helm's hand, and admit wryly that we never quite made it to the beach for surfing. Then we dashed back to our room, peeled off our clothes hurriedly, and loved each other through most of our last night in Maui.

The following afternoon, we boarded the plane home. Exhaustion caught up with me, and I slept most of the flight to LAX. Hayes, too. I felt refreshed by the time we picked up our luggage. So I lean in to kiss him, sure he'll come spend the night at my place. But Hayes simply carries my luggage up the stairs and to my door, then drops me off with a kiss.

"Hey, don't forget that Sunday movies and munchies is at my place at noon tomorrow. You'll be there, right?"

"Of course. Hayes—"

"Great. I'll see you then. Sleep good, shortcake."

He kisses my forehead and lopes down the stairs before I can call him back. Then he's gone.

I lock the door, frowning. There's no way our relationship was only a vacation fling. Right?

I'm still wondering the same thing when I wake Sunday morning, stretching after a fitful night of sleep. Why didn't Hayes stay with me? Sure, he hinted that he had some things to take care of after being gone.

Any chance he meant Jayci?

No, Hayes wouldn't intentionally hurt me like that.

Still, it's hard not to be insecure, especially when I glance at my phone. He hasn't left a single text or message since walking away.

Pensively, I shower and pick at some breakfast. My phone dings, and I jump for it. But it's just Maryam asking for a ride. There goes my idea of heading over to Hayes's place early to talk.

Sure. Pick you up at quarter to noon, I reply.

I should call Ella and Eryn. It's been over a week since I've talked to either of my sisters, which is totally unusual. But they're busy, and they knew I was in Hawaii. I have a couple of hours to kill. And maybe they'll have some advice on how to handle things when I see Hayes.

Ella's phone goes straight to voicemail. Maybe they're in church? It is Sunday morning, after all. But Eryn doesn't answer, either. Damn it. So much for the comfort of my sisters' sage advice.

I'll have to figure this out on my own.

I kill some time watching reruns of a favorite TV show, then head to my closet with a sigh. Decisions, decisions. The comfort of long skirts, oversized shirts, and Birkenstocks? Or the sex appeal of short skirts, high heels, and cleavage? Actually, the choice is easy. If Hayes thinks he can just come and go from my bed or that we're in any way done, I'm going to remind him of what he's not getting until he gets his shit together and talks to me.

Brimming with attitude, I pluck a daring orange dress off the hanger. The day Xavian talked me into it, I couldn't picture myself wearing anything that hugged me so tightly everyone can see the indentation of my belly button. The lycra dress barely covers the tops of my thighs. But the most daring part? Spaghetti straps cling to my shoulders while the buttons that hold the front of the dress together across my breasts strain, almost gaping to reveal the contents of my strapless bra. Hayes will take one look at this dress and flip.

How about that, pal?

After arranging my hair in a soft half up-half down 'do, I hop in my car and try my best to ignore the fact I'm shaking. And hopefully overreacting. Maybe Hayes just needed a night alone at his place to get it in order before everyone showed up today. Maybe I'm just being insecure after years of feeling invisible to him.

Either way, as I pull away from my apartment, Maryam texts to say that she doesn't need a ride after all because Graham unexpectedly picked her up on his way. But could I stop at the store for some champagne?

On it, I text back.

Weirdly, I bump into Kella at the store. "What are you doing here? I thought you'd already be at Hayes's place."

"Picking up some OJ for Graham." She scans me from head to toe, rearing back. "Wow, you look stunning."

Kella is no slouch herself, but she's complimenting me, so I smile. But I'm so confused. Why would the gang ask her to stop for OJ when I'm already here picking up champagne?

Whatever. I just want to get out of here and over to Hayes.

Kella stops me in the shampoo aisle. "Hang on. I'm looking for something new to try. Got recommendations? Your hair always looks amazing."

I give her some of my thoughts, but she seems to be half listening. And she's acting nervous.

"You okay?" I ask.

"Great." Her smile seems forced. "You?"

Confused as hell. "Fine."

And worried.

Does she know something I don't?

Suddenly, her phone dings. Her smile turns real, and she shrugs off her great shampoo dilemma. "I'll figure this out later. Let's go."

Kella all but drags me to the checkout counter and hustles through our purchases.

"What's going on?" I ask as we head to the lot, bombarded by a dry, relentlessly sunny day.

"Nothing." She shoots me another forced smile. "See you there!"

Before I can reply, she hops into her compact and peels away like she's on fire.

What the hell?

With a sigh and a niggle of worry that something weird is up, I settle into the driver's seat and drive the two miles to his place.

When I arrive at Hayes's bungalow, Kella has already parked and seemingly gone inside without me. In fact, no one is waiting outside for me, least of all the man I love.

Did I somehow misunderstand what our week in Hawaii meant to him?

Willing myself not to cry, I climb out of the car and take a deep breath. If Hayes acts like he's the same best buddy I had before we went to Maui, I'll smile my way through the movie, then stay after and ask him what the hell is going on. I don't want to lose him…but I don't know what I'll do if he breaks my heart.

Still, I can't fathom that. This must be some misunderstanding. Hayes has always been there for me.

As a friend. He's been a serial boyfriend to every other woman he's dated. Maybe you're just the latest?

Maybe, but I don't want to believe it. I have faith in him, in us. I have to…or what do we really have?

With a fortifying breath, I grab the champagne from the passenger's seat, along with my purse, then head to the front door, giving myself a pep talk. I love Hayes. He loves me. Whatever's going on, we'll talk it out. I'm not giving up.

Decision made, I ring the bell.

Hayes answers with a nervous smile, then he pulls me into the foyer, tugs me into his arms, and cups my face. "Damn, last night lasted forever. You look beautiful, and I'm doing everything out of order, but fuck it. I don't care."

Then he seizes my lips with his, plunging deep into my mouth and reminding me of the sugary, summery kisses he plied me with in Maui and lighting up my body like a firework.

When he finally comes up for air, I pull free and look around, surprised that we're alone. Where did everyone go? I don't understand, but that's not my most pressing question now. "Has something changed between us, Hayes?"

"Shortcake…" He turns solemn. "Everything has changed. Come inside. We should talk."

My stomach drops to my knees. Nerves rattle around the empty chasm as he leads me into the kitchen. There's food and drink everywhere, but it's strangely devoid of people. "What's going on? Where is everyone? Maryam and Kella are both acting weird, and you—"

"I'm nervous."

Because he needs reassurance about my feelings? Or because he's trying to find the right words to let me go? "Why?"

He takes my hands in his, takes my mouth with his. As he does, he clutches my heart even tighter in his grip. "I love you. I can't believe I overlooked you for so long. I feel like the stupidest ass on the planet. But you opened my eyes, and I see you so clearly. I want to spend my life with you. Please tell me you want to spend yours with me."

Then he kneels.

My heart jumps up to my throat. I gape and slap a hand over my mouth to cover my gasp. He's down on one knee? Surely I'm misunderstanding. Or hallucinating. Maybe the hours of positive projection have me seeing things I've only dreamed of.

"Hayes?" My voice shakes.

"Echo Annalise Hope, I fell in mad, passionate love with you last week, but it feels as if I've loved you forever. I don't want to go another day into my future without knowing you're mine. Would you make me beyond happy and marry me?"

Oh, my god, he's serious.

Hayes reaches into his pocket and pulls out a ring. He's totally serious. And the diamond he holds in his hand leaves me stunned. Set in rose gold, it looks vintage. The band is a collection of swirls and filigrees held together by tiny glimmering gems. The center stones have been arranged in the shape of a flower.

It looks like something he would have had made just for me because I can't imagine anything more perfect.

I don't have to think twice.

"Yes. Oh, my... Yes!" I start to cry.

Hayes leaps to his feet, hauls me in his arms, and crushes my lips under his in celebration. He's already stolen my heart, but when I'm in his arms, he steals my breath and my mind, too.

"Did she say yes?" Kella demands from the back bedroom.

My fiancé—it seems crazy to think that—reluctantly ends our kiss and lifts his head. "Yes. You can all come out now."

What is going on?

I turn to see our friends file into the kitchen wearing huge smiles, then I whirl back on Hayes. "They were in on this?"

"Everyone was. From the minute I dropped you off at your apartment last night, looking so confused and forlorn until now, yes. I wanted today to be perfect for you. For us."

"I never expected anything like this." And the fact that he not only proposed, but put so much thought into making this moment one we'll both remember has me tearing up with joy. "Thank you."

"You never have to thank me, shortcake. Just love me."

"Always." I cup his face, amazed and thrilled that I'll be spending my life with my very best friend.

"There's more," he whispers, pointing to something behind me.

I turn again to see Ella and Eryn bustle into the living room beside their husbands with huge grins on their faces.

With a shriek, I jump up and down, then turn to Hayes again. "You did this?"

"I called them on Wednesday to tell them I intended to propose. They wanted to be here, and I wanted them here for you."

Hayes could have proposed in Maui, and some people might have thought that would be far more romantic, but he understands how much my sisters mean to me, and his thoughtfulness fills my heart.

I rush to hug my sisters, who squee and hug me back with equal fervor. "You're here!"

"We are." Eryn grips my hands. "I just knew there was more than friendship between you two. Congratulations!"

"Thanks." I try not to cry fat tears of joy, but it's hopeless.

Best. Day. Ever.

Especially when Ella grabs me in a hug. "You're going to be a bride. I'm so thrilled for you."

She's right. Yikes! "I have a lot of planning to do." Not my forte. "Will you help me?"

Ella is so much more organized.

She smiles. "I'll do my best."

Of course it won't be easy. "North Carolina is a long way away, and you're busy with work—"

"That's not all." She slides a hand over her still-flat stomach. "You're going to be an aunt before Christmas."

"Seriously?" I hug her close again. "Oh, my god! I'm so excited for you. Both of you." I step into her husband Carson's arms for a brotherly hug. "Congratulations! You'll be the best parents ever."

Certainly way better than we had as kids. I don't even ask if my parents know about this event. It doesn't matter because they proved long ago that they don't care about anything except work and each other. I've come to peace with that. I have my sisters, Hayes, and soon a niece or nephew. I have everything I need.

Eryn and her husband, West, exchange a glance before he clears his throat and flashes my middle sister a secretive grin. "We're expecting a baby, too. Around New Year's. We just found out Friday."

Screw trying to stop the tears. They flow down my face. My sisters' faces, too, as we dogpile into a hug full of joy, sniffles, laughs, and well wishes.

Hayes sidles behind me again, cupping my shoulders softly. "Someone else wants to congratulate you."

I look up to find Gramma Liddy balanced between Graham and Xavian. She looks a little older and a little frailer than the last time I saw her, but having her here to celebrate with us is so unexpected and special.

I sprint to hug the tiny older woman who's smiling from ear to ear. "You came, too? Thank you so much!"

"Hayes insisted. I wouldn't have missed it for the world since I've been telling him for the last half dozen years to marry you. I'm thrilled you said yes." She studies me with misty blue eyes. "Like you, he didn't have the best family growing up, but you'll make a new family together. And I know you'll make each other so happy."

"We will," I promise. Then I turn to Xavian. "I didn't expect you to fly back from Maui."

"I had to see two of my favorite people get engaged." He mock punches Hayes in the chest. "Besides, he wasn't going to stop threatening to beat the living shit out of me until I promised to stop meddling between him and his woman. And I forgot what you looked like in all the bikinis and lingerie I helped you pick out."

Collectively, everyone laughs, including Hayes. I'm turning ten shades of red, but I hug Xavian tight. "None of this would have happened without you. Thanks for going out on a limb to help me. I'm forever grateful."

"It would have happened. Maybe not as fast…" He shrugs like it's no big deal, but I know better. "Someday you can return the favor."

"If you ever need advice—or anything—I'm always here for you. I'll miss having you nearby, but just pick up the phone."

"Will do. But…I also came because it was my turn to pick today's movie." He winks.

Then the festivities start in earnest, kicking off with the strains of Maroon 5's upbeat romantic ballad "Sugar." The day is full of fun, food, champagne, good cheer, and utter perfection. Hours later, our friends leave with waves and well wishes. My sisters and their husbands head back to their hotel, promising to have lunch with Hayes and me tomorrow. Liddy disappears to the guest bedroom to nap.

Finally, I'm alone with the man I love. The man who's been my best friend for most of my life. The man I'm going to marry.

"Happy, shortcake?"

I turn to him with a smile that won't quit. "Sublimely. Think we have time to sneak into your bedroom so I can show you how much?"

"We'll always make time for that." He sets a hand at the small of my back and ushers me into his bedroom, shutting the door behind us. "I knew there was a reason I loved you."

"You didn't always."

"I did. I was just too dumb to see it. Forgive me?"

"I already have." I press my lips to his. "When should we get married? Ella mentioned planning, and I nearly broke out in hives. It's so overwhelming…"

"Don't panic. I thought you might feel that way, so I called Keeley. She's got an opening to get married on the bed-and-breakfast's front lawn, facing the ocean, in about three weeks. I know you've always wanted to get married barefoot. Being a June bride is pretty traditional for you, but I thought getting married in the place we first fell in love would be great. What do you say?"

The day has already been so full of amazing bliss, it's hard to believe I can still cry more tears of joy. "It sounds perfect. Just like you, string bean."

"No one is more perfect than you. I can't wait to make you Mrs. Echo Elliot. But maybe you want me to nibble on my very favorite shortcake right now?"

"Oh, I do."

He gives a whoop, then kisses me with his whole heart. We melt together, starting our shimmering, perfect future in each other's arms.

Want to know more about sharky Sebastian Shaw sleeping with the enemy? Read the juicy enemies-to-lovers Reed Family novel, MORE THAN HATE YOU!

* * * *

Also from 1001 Dark Nights and Shayla Black, discover Forever Wicked, Pure Wicked, Dirty Wicked, More Than Pleasure You, and More Than Protect You.

Sign up for the 1001 Dark Nights Newsletter
and be entered to win a Tiffany Key necklace.

There's a contest every month!

Go to www.1001DarkNights.com to subscribe.

**As a bonus, all subscribers can download
FIVE FREE exclusive books!**

Discover 1001 Dark Nights Collection Eight

DRAGON REVEALED by Donna Grant
A Dragon Kings Novella

CAPTURED IN INK by Carrie Ann Ryan
A Montgomery Ink: Boulder Novella

SECURING JANE by Susan Stoker
A SEAL of Protection: Legacy Series Novella

WILD WIND by Kristen Ashley
A Chaos Novella

DARE TO TEASE by Carly Phillips
A Dare Nation Novella

VAMPIRE by Rebecca Zanetti
A Dark Protectors/Rebels Novella

MAFIA KING by Rachel Van Dyken
A Mafia Royals Novella

THE GRAVEDIGGER'S SON by Darynda Jones
A Charley Davidson Novella

FINALE by Skye Warren
A North Security Novella

MEMORIES OF YOU by J. Kenner
A Stark Securities Novella

SLAYED BY DARKNESS by Alexandra Ivy
A Guardians of Eternity Novella

TREASURED by Lexi Blake
A Masters and Mercenaries Novella

THE DAREDEVIL by Dylan Allen
A Rivers Wilde Novella

BOND OF DESTINY by Larissa Ione
A Demonica Novella

THE CLOSE-UP by Kennedy Ryan
A Hollywood Renaissance Novella

MORE THAN POSSESS YOU by Shayla Black
A More Than Words Novella

HAUNTED HOUSE by Heather Graham
A Krewe of Hunters Novella

MAN FOR ME by Laurelin Paige
A Man In Charge Novella

THE RHYTHM METHOD by Kylie Scott
A Stage Dive Novella

JONAH BENNETT by Tijan
A Bennett Mafia Novella

CHANGE WITH ME by Kristen Proby
A With Me In Seattle Novella

THE DARKEST DESTINY by Gena Showalter
A Lords of the Underworld Novella

Also from Blue Box Press

THE LAST TIARA by M.J. Rose

THE CROWN OF GILDED BONES by Jennifer L. Armentrout
A Blood and Ash Novel

THE MISSING SISTER by Lucinda Riley

THE END OF FOREVER by Steve Berry and M.J. Rose
A Cassiopeia Vitt Adventure

THE STEAL by C. W. Gortner and M.J. Rose

CHASING SERENITY by Kristen Ashley
A River Rain Novel

A SHADOW IN THE EMBER by Jennifer L. Armentrout
A Flesh and Fire Novel

Discover More Shayla Black

More Than Protect You
A More Than Words Novella

Can I keep the gorgeous, gun-shy single mother safe—and prove I'm the man for her?

I'm Tanner Kirk—Certified firearms instructor and mixed martial arts enthusiast. When I filed for divorce at the end of an empty marriage, all I wanted was a vacation in paradise, not another woman in my life. But how can I possibly say no to Amanda Lund, a young single mom desperate to learn self-defense? Or refuse the banked desire on the guarded beauty's face?

I can't.

So I seduce Mandy until we're burning up the sheets…and soon find my heart entangled with her bruised and battered one. But when a nemesis from her past tries to destroy our future by unearthing my secret, will she understand and forgive me—or give up on us forever?

* * * *

More Than Pleasure You
A More Than Words Novella

Can I convince her our hot but temporary engagement should last forever?

I'm Stephen Lund, confirmed bachelor…and son of a successful billionaire whose sins I can't forget—or forgive. Though he insisted I get over his transgressions, I can't. So I put space between us with a temporary getaway to Maui. My rental's sexy caretaker, Skye Ingram, is a beautiful distraction. Yeah, it's a terrible time to start a fling, but I can't help wanting to give her every bit of pleasure she's willing to take.

When Skye needs a date to her ex-boyfriend's wedding, I'm game to play her pretend fiancé. The jerk should see what he passed up…and that I'm holding her now. But our pretend engagement begins to feel real. Our passion certainly is. So are the consequences. When I'm confronted with the reality that our lives are now irrevocably entwined, I have to choose between leaving Skye to return to the life—and wealth—I've always known or abandoning everything familiar to start over with the woman who awakened my heart.

* * * *

Dirty Wicked
A Wicked Lovers Novella

After being framed for a crime he didn't commit, former private eye Nick Navarro has nothing but revenge on his mind—until a woman from his past returns to beg for his help.

Beautiful widow Sasha Porter has been hunted by his enemies. Desperate, she offers him anything to keep her young daughter safe, even agreeing to become his mistress. The last thing either of them want are emotional entanglements but as they entrap the ruthless politician who arranged Nick's downfall and passion sizzles between them, danger closes in.

Will he choose love over vengeance before it's too late?

* * * *

Pure Wicked
A Wicked Lovers Novella

During his decade as an international pop star, Jesse McCall has lived every day in the fast lane. A committed hedonist reveling in amazing highs, globetrotting, and nameless encounters, he refuses to think about his loneliness or empty future. Then tragedy strikes.

Shocked and grieving, he sheds his identity and walks away, searching for peace. Instead, he finds Bristol Reese, a no-nonsense beauty scraping to keep her business afloat while struggling with her own demons. He's intent on seducing her, but other than a pleasure-filled night, she's not interested in a player, especially after her boyfriend recently proposed to her sister. In order to claim Bristol, Jesse has to prove he's not the kind of man he's always been. But when she learns his identity and his past comes back to haunt him, how will he convince her that he's a changed man who wants nothing more than to make her his forever?

* * * *

Forever Wicked
A Wicked Lovers Novella

They had nothing in common but a desperate passion…

Billionaire Jason Denning lived life fast and hard in a world where anything could be bought and sold, even affection. But all that changed when he met "Greta," a beautiful stranger ready to explore her hidden desires. From a blue collar family, Gia Angelotti wore a badge, fought for right—and opened herself utterly to love him. Blindsided and falling hard, Jason does the first impulsive thing of his life and hustles her to the altar.

Until a second chance proved that forever could be theirs.

Then tragedy ripped Jason's new bride from his arms and out of his life. When he finds Gia again, he gives her a choice: spend the three weeks before their first anniversary with him or forfeit the money she receives from their marriage. Reluctantly, she agrees to once again put herself at his mercy and return to his bed. But having her right where he wants her is dangerous for Jason's peace of mind. No matter how hard he tries, he finds himself falling for her again. Will he learn to trust that their love is real before Gia leaves again for good?

More Than Hate You

Reed Family Reckoning: Friends, Book 7
By Shayla Black
Coming November 9, 2021

I seduced her to close the deal. Now I refuse to ever let her go.

I'm Sebastian Shaw—CFO, pragmatist, and dealmaker. The only thing I've ever mismanaged is love, but a decade in business has proven I can successfully negotiate with anyone…except the irrationally stubborn O'Neills. After their patriarch's sudden retirement, I find myself sparring long-distance over a make-or-break merger with his youngest daughter, Sloan. She's a ball-busting piece of work. Thankfully, I have skills, an hourglass-shaped stranger I recently met to relieve my stress, and a killer plan to take down my rival.

Then I realize the gorgeous distraction in my bed is Sloan. Worse, I'm falling for her.

Suddenly, everything from my objectives to my morals is cloudy. Stay loyal to my best friend and boss to get this critical deal done at any cost…or give my heart another chance? But the more time I spend with Sloan O'Neill, the more I realize she's sharp, determined, funny, and kind of perfect for me. She has no idea how far I'll go to mend this rift and make her mine—but she's about to find out.

* * * *

Sloan sighs again, this time even harder. "Screw it. I'm pouring a glass of wine."

"Sounds like you could use it."

After some rustling sounds, I hear the soft pop of a cork, followed by the clink of a glass. Liquid splashing follows. Then she sips and swallows.

"Better?" I ask.

"I wish. I don't usually open wine on a Monday, but I want to shake all these VPs. After you and I talked on Friday night, I spent the weekend scouring that annual report. We should be in a far more liquid position than we are. Mr. Rawson wouldn't be happy that his son is financing these secret projects and potentially jeopardizing the organization's cash position. Frankly, more than one department is relying on improved funding next year. The R and D people alone need a boatload of money to keep up with those cutthroats over at Stratus."

Cutthroats? We're simply smart players, damn it. "They're competitors, right?"

"They're more than that. For years, we had this unspoken line in the sand. They handled the large-business market, so it made sense for them to have all these redundant, off-site servers for storing data. We catered to the home office and very small-business audience. So our on-site solutions, especially with the advances in technology from magnetic to solid state drives, made sense for those customers. We only serviced a sizable business if they approached us first. But what did Lucifer—I mean, Evan Cook—and that swaggering asshole of a sidekick"—She snaps her fingers. "I can't think of his name."

She means me. "Asshole?"

"Yeah. He's their CFO, technically. But he's pretty much their corporate mouthpiece. Cook doesn't like to make speeches, attend tech conferences, or give interviews for industry press, so this guy does it for him. He gave a presentation at an event I attended a few years back. He clearly likes to hear himself talk. Thank god I was at the back of the room, and I could leave almost as soon as it began. But you know what the asshole did?"

Came after the home-and-small-business market—like any good businessperson with two brain cells to rub together would. Evan and Stratus didn't need Rawson's or Sloan's permission to do that. "What?"

"Jumped into our arena without warning. Full product suite, competitive pricing, ads up the ass…"

"And you weren't happy about it?"

She scoffs. "Why come after our customers before improving the market penetration with their own first? It's a threat to our bottom line, frankly at the worst possible time. And now Reservoir's disappearing funds threaten to undo us altogether. And I'm the only one warning management that the sky is falling. I don't understand."

"First of all, don't sweat Stratus. Competition happens, and all you can do is try to compete. Reservoir is doing a good job," I have to admit. "From the conversations I had with Bruce Rawson before he hired me"—well, from my own research, but whatever—"they're holding their own in their original market segment while making inroads in the large-business market."

"*Modest* inroads," she corrects.

"It hasn't been that long, and an on-site storage solution isn't right for a lot of bigger companies, especially those with multiple branches or offices."

"How would you know that?"

I wince. I've got to be fucking careful not to give my identity—and my whole scheme—away. "You're not the only one who's been doing their homework lately. Part of my effort to help you is to understand your industry and what's going on."

"Of course. You're right. I'm not thinking."

"Still mad at Lucifer's swaggering asshole of a sidekick?"

"I'd love to crush him. It's on my to-do list." She swallows back more wine. "But right now, I'm focused on all the VPs and their terrible stewardship of our corporate funds."

Seriously, why doesn't she just call her father and tell him what's going on, maybe get his advice? I'm not sure, and that's not my problem. Maybe my swagger and I can step in to fill the void.

"The org charts don't indicate there's anyone else you can take this to. Well, unless you think the comptroller has balls."

"Our comptroller is a woman, so she doesn't."

"I don't mean that literally. You're a woman, and you have balls."

"You think so?" She sounds touched by my opinion.

"Hell yeah." In fact, I'm hard-pressed to think of many women with as much moxie as Sloan. Nia comes to mind. Evan's sisters, Harlow and Bethany, for sure. I admire all of them.

On Sloan, drive and guts are sexy in a way that has nothing to do with physical beauty. I barely know what she looks like, but I'd absolutely fuck her with a smile on my face.

"Thanks. That means a lot to me. Unfortunately, Anna doesn't have metaphorical balls, either. So I don't know what to do. Besides, she reports up to Brenda Keller."

Who would probably tell her not to talk. Sloan is in a bad spot, and I need to help her so she can help me. The key to understanding how to keep Reservoir from pitching to Wyman is to understand what the fuck is going on with the company financially.

Then inspiration strikes, mostly because I've used this tactic a time or two. "Have you tried approaching the VPs' assistants? Not the directors or managers who report to them but their admins?"

"No, but that's brilliant. I know Perez's assistant, Carissa, is getting married, but her girl tribe is out east in Kilgore, so she's feeling alone and stressed in the big city. I could invite her for a girls' night and see what she knows."

"Exactly. The worst that can happen is you find out she's clueless, but at least you'll have had a good time and maybe made a connection." At least that was always my philosophy when I used to schmooze girls in college for help with tests and term papers. We'd study together while hooking up, so they were happy to help me. When the project or class was over, we would be, too. None of them ever seemed butt-hurt, and I always did my best to leave them with a smile.

"I like it. If I strike out there, I'll try someone else. Smith's admin is his sister, so I don't think I'll get anywhere with her, but Roop's is this guy named Ryan, who just moved to town."

Instantly, I picture her with some handsy player, and I scowl. "You don't have to compromise your ethics."

"By doing what, sleeping with him?" She gives me a soft little laugh. "First, I wouldn't. Second, I'm pretty sure he's gay. He keeps a Henry Cavill calendar in his office, tucked discreetly where no one walking by can see it, but it's there."

That makes me breathe a sigh of relief. Then I tell myself to stop being ridiculous. I shouldn't care if this woman I've never even met spends her downtime getting horizontal with a guy.

But I do.

If Sloan didn't work for Reservoir, and if I wasn't the swaggering asshole-ish sidekick of Satan gainfully employed by their competitor…and deceiving her for purely business reasons, I think we'd get along. Hell, we have chemistry. I bet we'd have amazing sex…

About Shayla Black

LET'S GET TO KNOW EACH OTHER!

ABOUT ME:

Shayla Black is the *New York Times* and *USA Today* bestselling author of over eighty novels. For twenty years, she's written contemporary, erotic, paranormal, and historical romances via traditional, independent, foreign, and audio publishers. Her books have sold millions of copies and been published in a dozen languages.

Raised an only child, Shayla occupied herself with lots of daydreaming, much to the chagrin of her teachers. In college, she found her love for reading and realized that she could have a career publishing the stories spinning in her imagination. Though she graduated with a degree in Marketing/Advertising and embarked on a stint in corporate America to pay the bills, her heart has always been with her characters. She's thrilled that she's been living her dream as a full-time author for the past eleven years.

Shayla currently lives in North Texas with her wonderfully supportive husband and daughter, as well as two spoiled tabbies. In her "free" time, she enjoys reality TV, reading, and listening to an eclectic blend of music.

TELL ME MORE ABOUT YOU.

The VIP Readers newsletter has exclusive news and excerpts. You can also become one of my Facebook Book Beauties and enjoy live, interactive #WineWednesday video chats full of fun, book chatter, and more! See you soon!

Connect with me online:

Website: http://shaylablack.com

VIP Reader Newsletter: http://shayla.link/nwsltr

Facebook Author Page: http://shayla.link/FBPage

Facebook Book Beauties Chat Group: http://shayla.link/FBChat

Instagram: https://instagram.com/ShaylaBlack/

TikTok: www.tiktok.com/@shayla_black

Book+Main: http://shayla.link/books+main

Twitter: http://twitter.com/ShaylaBlackAuth

Amazon Author Page: http://shayla.link/AmazonFollow
BookBub: http://shayla.link/BookBub
Goodreads: http://shayla.link/goodreads
YouTube: http://shayla.link/youtube

Discover 1001 Dark Nights

COLLECTION ONE
FOREVER WICKED by Shayla Black ~ CRIMSON TWILIGHT by
Heather Graham ~ CAPTURED IN SURRENDER by Liliana Hart ~
SILENT BITE: A SCANGUARDS WEDDING by Tina Folsom ~
DUNGEON GAMES by Lexi Blake ~ AZAGOTH by Larissa Ione ~
NEED YOU NOW by Lisa Renee Jones ~ SHOW ME, BABY by
Cherise Sinclair~ ROPED IN by Lorelei James ~ TEMPTED BY
MIDNIGHT by Lara Adrian ~ THE FLAME by Christopher Rice ~
CARESS OF DARKNESS by Julie Kenner

COLLECTION TWO
WICKED WOLF by Carrie Ann Ryan ~ WHEN IRISH EYES ARE
HAUNTING by Heather Graham ~ EASY WITH YOU by Kristen
Proby ~ MASTER OF FREEDOM by Cherise Sinclair ~ CARESS OF
PLEASURE by Julie Kenner ~ ADORED by Lexi Blake ~ HADES by
Larissa Ione ~ RAVAGED by Elisabeth Naughton ~ DREAM OF YOU
by Jennifer L. Armentrout ~ STRIPPED DOWN by Lorelei James ~
RAGE/KILLIAN by Alexandra Ivy/Laura Wright ~ DRAGON KING
by Donna Grant ~ PURE WICKED by Shayla Black ~ HARD AS
STEEL by Laura Kaye ~ STROKE OF MIDNIGHT by Lara Adrian ~
ALL HALLOWS EVE by Heather Graham ~ KISS THE FLAME by
Christopher Rice~ DARING HER LOVE by Melissa Foster ~ TEASED
by Rebecca Zanetti ~ THE PROMISE OF SURRENDER by Liliana
Hart

COLLECTION THREE
HIDDEN INK by Carrie Ann Ryan ~ BLOOD ON THE BAYOU by
Heather Graham ~ SEARCHING FOR MINE by Jennifer Probst ~
DANCE OF DESIRE by Christopher Rice ~ ROUGH RHYTHM by
Tessa Bailey ~ DEVOTED by Lexi Blake ~ Z by Larissa Ione ~
FALLING UNDER YOU by Laurelin Paige ~ EASY FOR KEEPS by
Kristen Proby ~ UNCHAINED by Elisabeth Naughton ~ HARD TO
SERVE by Laura Kaye ~ DRAGON FEVER by Donna Grant ~
KAYDEN/SIMON by Alexandra Ivy/Laura Wright ~ STRUNG UP by
Lorelei James ~ MIDNIGHT UNTAMED by Lara Adrian ~ TRICKED
by Rebecca Zanetti ~ DIRTY WICKED by Shayla Black ~ THE ONLY
ONE by Lauren Blakely ~ SWEET SURRENDER by Liliana Hart

ABANDON by Rachel Van Dyken ~ THE OPEN DOOR by Laurelin Paige ~ CLOSER by Kylie Scott ~ SOMETHING JUST LIKE THIS by Jennifer Probst ~ BLOOD NIGHT by Heather Graham ~ TWIST OF FATE by Jill Shalvis ~ MORE THAN PLEASURE YOU by Shayla Black ~ WONDER WITH ME by Kristen Proby ~ THE DARKEST ASSASSIN by Gena Showalter

COLLECTION SEVEN
THE BISHOP by Skye Warren ~ TAKEN WITH YOU by Carrie Ann Ryan ~ DRAGON LOST by Donna Grant ~ SEXY LOVE by Carly Phillips ~ PROVOKE by Rachel Van Dyken ~ RAFE by Sawyer Bennett ~ THE NAUGHTY PRINCESS by Claire Contreras ~ THE GRAVEYARD SHIFT by Darynda Jones ~ CHARMED by Lexi Blake ~ SACRIFICE OF DARKNESS by Alexandra Ivy ~ THE QUEEN by Jen Armentrout ~ BEGIN AGAIN by Jennifer Probst ~ VIXEN by Rebecca Zanetti ~ SLASH by Laurelin Paige ~ THE DEAD HEAT OF SUMMER by Heather Graham ~ WILD FIRE by Kristen Ashley ~ MORE THAN PROTECT YOU by Shayla Black ~ LOVE SONG by Kylie Scott ~ CHERISH ME by J. Kenner ~ SHINE WITH ME by Kristen Proby

Discover Blue Box Press
TAME ME by J. Kenner ~ TEMPT ME by J. Kenner ~ DAMIEN by J. Kenner ~ TEASE ME by J. Kenner ~ REAPER by Larissa Ione ~ THE SURRENDER GATE by Christopher Rice ~ SERVICING THE TARGET by Cherise Sinclair ~ THE LAKE OF LEARNING by Steve Berry and MJ Rose ~ THE MUSEUM OF MYSTERIES by Steve Berry and MJ Rose ~ TEASE ME by J. Kenner ~ FROM BLOOD AND ASH by Jennifer L. Armentrout ~ QUEEN MOVE by Kennedy Ryan ~ THE HOUSE OF LONG AGO by Steve Berry and MJ Rose ~ THE BUTTERFLY ROOM by Lucinda Riley ~ A KINGDOM OF FLESH AND FIRE by Jennifer L. Armentrout

On Behalf of 1001 Dark Nights,

Liz Berry, M.J. Rose, and Jillian Stein would like to thank ~

Steve Berry
Doug Scofield
Benjamin Stein
Kim Guidroz
Social Butterfly PR
Ashley Wells
Asha Hossain
Chris Graham
Chelle Olson
Kasi Alexander
Jessica Johns
Dylan Stockton
Richard Blake
and Simon Lipskar

Made in the USA
Coppell, TX
22 September 2021